The Quick

The Quick

stories

Barbara Scott

CORMORANT
BOOKS

The publisher gratefully acknowledges the support of the Canada Council for the Arts and the Ontario Arts Council for its publishing program. We acknowledge the financial support of the Government of Canada through the Book Publishing Industry Development Program (BPIDP) for our publishing activities.

Canada

THE CANADA COUNCIL | LE CONSEIL DES ARTS
FOR THE ARTS | DU CANADA
SINCE 1957 | DEPUIS 1957

Canadian Cataloguing in Publication Data
Scott, Barbara, 1957-
The quick
ISBN 1-896951-17-1
I. Title.
PS8587.C619Q85 1999   C813'.54   C99-900955-9
PR9199.3.S318Q85 1999
Printed in Canada.

CORMORANT BOOKS INC.
RR 1, Dunvegan, ON K0C 1J0

In memory of
George Scott 1924–1994
Brenda Hryhor 1951–1995

For Keith
and for my family

Contents

ORANGES

In my grandmother's kitchen there are no Ukrainian Easter eggs, their geometric lines poking fun at perfect ovarian curves; no orthodox icons in a sensuous riot of colour mocking any attempt at strict asceticism. There are no traces of Ukrainian costume; those glorious colours and streamers are never seen, not even on special days. It was all my grandmother could do to trade in her pilled-over brown rayon pants and green acrylic sweater for a sagging green wool skirt and a navy cotton shell before heading to bingo on Wednesday nights.

On the sideboard in my grandmother's kitchen, children and grandchildren are framed in cardboard, grey, navy and black. There are no shiny appliances on the counters, no spots on the speckled linoleum. No wooden plaques with rhyming kitchen prayers on the walls, no coiled throw rugs on the floor. It is a kitchen marked by absence, bare of decoration, bare of colour, bare of all that could be called bohunk.

The strongest surviving presence in my grandmother's kitchen, now that my grandmother is no longer there herself, is the smell of food — the holubtsi, pyrohy, kielbasa, sauerkraut soup and borscht that we heated up yesterday. She had enough food in the fridge, freezer and pantry to take care of her own wake. She would have been proud.

The wake was yesterday. Today, my mother and I inhale the fading aromas, and finish washing up the dishes. The chrome sink gleams; the dishtowel — folded neatly in thirds, not in half — hangs with edges trim under the sink. The last time the three of us were here together, I watched with open mouth as my grandmother elbowed my mother aside, "Out of the way, Karolka, I can do it better myself." The source of tradition, a piece of the puzzle locking into place, the same words ringing down long years of my childhood, but from my mother to me. This kitchen is also where I learned the source of another tradition: my habit of paring potatoes so stingily you can see through the peels. It is a custom born in the Depression, useless to cling to now, but I remember my pride on the day I first held a slender shaving to my own kitchen window in Vancouver, first saw that murky glimmer. My grandmother's smile.

My mother sits at the kitchen table, peeling an orange; breathes from a clear green plastic tube that coils from her nostrils and hooks her up to a black box twenty feet away that chortles and chugs and keeps her oxygen levels high enough to sustain life. We have been looking at photos; the cheap plastic cases are spread over the table. "When I was young...," she says. And I lean my elbows on the table while she talks past the phlegm in her lungs and mouth, past the tubes in her nose. "When I was young," she says, "I loved oranges even better than candy. You couldn't get them more than a couple of times a year in Kelvington during the Depression, and even then my family could never afford them. I didn't taste one until I was seven, and I thought it was the most wonderful flavour in the world. Later on, though, I discovered tomato sandwiches."

When he read the first ten pages of the family history my mother wrote for the Kelvington town history book, my husband, Leon, who is at the funeral parlour settling the last few details, said, "I don't know. It's just a bunch of detail with nothing *behind* it. I don't get a sense of where you come from, what your background is, who your people were." My people. Sounds like Bostonians with several generations of gracious living behind them, not like the Ukrainian immigrants who scratched out a living in the dustbowl of Saskatchewan. This is the kind of cliché my mind slides into whenever I think back to the infrequent stories my mother has told me. They scroll before me in black and white or sepia, not like those art movies that load every shadow with meaning but like the photos on the table — flat, with a scratchy finish. My grandfather is Henry Fonda, with jutting chin and stoic bearing, my whole family stiff with peasant dignity — the Joads, but with Ukrainian accents. They stare into colourless sunsets and angle-park by the drugstore in clouds of grey dust. In my mind the drugstore always has faded wooden boards curled by the dust and dry heat, and inside my mother is always thirteen, wearing a scratchy flour-sack dress. She too is in black and white. But the tomato sandwich frozen halfway to her mouth drips red juice and one yellow seed onto the smooth grey countertop.

When Leon says, "your people," so pat, so easy, I see a family history whole and entire, custom-wrapped and handed down like an heirloom, something rare, to be handled reverently, with love. When Leon says, "your people," I see *his* people, and I think, "Easy for you," coming from that long line of born storytellers. My family hand down nothing whole and entire. Like the photographs, they offer to the world and to me only the smooth face of an eternally trapped present. But occasionally the flat surface buckles and tears, occasionally it lets things slip, so that my history is something I have had to put together piece by piece, segment by segment.

Spirals of orange peel wind over my mother's knuckles, drop over her wrist to the Arborite table. She has lovely hands, fine-boned with delicate nails, and her skin, loosened by age, sits so lightly on those bones you could almost believe yourself capable, if you dared, of peeling it away in pliant sheets, of tracing the bright red pumping of arteries, the blue tangle of nerves. "The first time I ever tasted an orange," she says, "was in the late part of the Depression. When your grandparents were running the store on Main Street with your great-uncle Nick and his wife, my Auntie Daisy. Your grandma's sister, she was. I wouldn't have been more than seven. They kept a canning jar on the top shelf for spare coin. No one ever took money out of that jar without all four adults agreeing to it. It was a communal jar, and all decisions made concerning it had to be communal. This was mostly your grandfather's influence, of course, coming out of his commitment to Marxism. Anyway, there I was in the grey wool bathrobe that was all I had for a winter jacket, and the rubber boots that were all I had for shoes. The boots were so big I had to wear three layers of your grandfather's grey work socks to keep them from falling off. Of course, there were care parcels from the Red Cross, but somehow the stuff inside never made it from the English families, who all knew the railway worker Mr. Thomas, to the bohunks across the tracks.

"December first, a box of oranges arrived at the store. A kind of miracle, especially at that time of year. They cost ten cents each. More than a loaf of bread. Mrs. Thomas came in with her daughter Jennifer in their fur collars and button-up boots and bought a dozen. Your grandmother watched them leave with the oranges, and then she looked at me. All week all we had eaten was baked potatoes with the skins on and some homemade cottage cheese. She did what she could to give the meal extra flavour by sprinkling it with the dill that she kept layered with salt and frozen in a jar by the back door. All the same, I was staring so hard at those oranges my stomach hurt. And she gave me one. Paid for it, too, by stealing a dime right out of the jar."

And I can see it all: pint-sized canning jar, with a red rubber sealing ring and glass lid and the raised letters in bubbles of glass on the sides. The pile of coins, their slow and painful pilgrimage towards the rim. Pennies mostly, from bright coppers to greenish-black lumps, but sometimes a nickel or even a dime flashing a defiant silver from beneath layers of grimy tarnish. I see the oranges, each in its wrapping of tissue paper, the smell a wild and sweet possession. Her mother packs them, one by one, into a brown paper bag, and the other woman scoops the bag under her arm, handing an orange, carelessly perhaps, to her daughter. The door opens and slams; a wedge of light and a cold blast of air cut across the worn floorboards and are gone. My mother's rubber boots scuff the bare wood floor; her eyes, wet with longing, are fixed on the fruit's warm glow. She is the little match girl staring through a frosted pane, Lillian Gish locked out in the snow.

Her mother's face like ice when it has frozen too fast and cracked. The lines waver, shift, harden. She reaches one hand for the jar, the other at her lips to keep her daughter quiet. The ring of the till, the rustle of sweet-scented paper. And then an orange is smooth and heavy in a fine-boned hand, and tangy and sweet on an urgent tongue. And for a moment — quick, before it vanishes — I am there too, awkward in the grey wool bathrobe that is two sizes too small for me, reaching for the peel drying in the sagging pocket. Never quite touching.

"For the longest time, whenever I tasted an orange, I could see her hand reaching for the jar." My mother's eyes are fixed on the orange, her fingers toy with the scraps of peel before her. "Your grandfather was very angry when he found out, her going behind his back like that." She pauses. "They never really were suited to one another. He was an intellectual. She loved to garden and can and had no time to talk. She and I would spend all day in the kitchen, making pyrohy." There they are, cutting out perfect rounds of soft pyrohy dough with a glass, pressing a mound of warm potato mashed with cottage cheese into the centre, then crimping the edges to form warm, soft pillows. "Then your grandpa's friends would come over at night and eat them with melted butter and onion. I remember sitting at the table with your grandfather and his friends, listening to them talk politics, government, revolution." Feel the fists banging the table, see the golden butter drizzling down their chins. "Sometimes they let me eat with them — back then I could eat twenty pyrohies at a sitting, for all I was only five feet tall and just out of the San, with one lung lost to TB."

My mother adored him, you can see it even now in the slight tremble of lip, glisten of eye. There she sits at the table laden with food, sits not with the men but slightly off to one side so that she can stare undisturbed at his animated face. They are freedom fighters, firm of chin and stern of eye. And she glows with their reflected glory, like Ingrid Bergman, all misty with emotion and soft light. And my grandmother? Perhaps that is her at the stove, with her back turned. Or maybe that is her in shadow, watching from the doorframe.

My mother lifts the pale green hose from her nostrils, wipes her nose with a tissue, returns the hose. "Your grandmother never wanted to marry your grandfather. She wanted to go to high school, she was only fifteen. But they were living in a two-room house. A shack, really, I've seen pictures of it. There simply was no money for food and clothing, let alone for school. She was the oldest of four children. It was just easier for her parents if she got married. And so she did. Of course, your grandmother didn't tell me any of this. Auntie Daisy told me. She thought I should know."

The last time I saw my grandfather he pulled me onto his knee, where I perched awkwardly, afraid to let him bear my full weight. I was fifteen. He was crying. He hadn't seen me for three years. Over and over he said, "Honest to God I cry, Blane, honest to God." Sometimes I can still feel the scratch of his beard against my neck. But then I only wanted to get away from the crush of his embrace.

The only time I saw my mother cry was on the long drive

home from Kelvington to Calgary after my grandfather's funeral. We stopped to see my grandmother on our way out of town, and as my mother told her about the service my grandmother's face was all bone. Nothing pliant to shift or waver, nothing to see behind. Two hours out of Kelvington my mother pulled over and stopped the car, crying into the steering wheel with the hoarse sobs of someone unused to crying. "God, doesn't she feel anything? I'm so afraid I'll end up like her. Dead. Just dead." But when I put my hand on her arm, she snatched it away and started the engine, scrubbing roughly at her face.

"He wasn't a bad man," my mother says, more to herself than to me. "But times were so hard then. My aunt once told me that when they first got married your grandma used to paint the Ukrainian Easter eggs, that she had a whole basket of them, all in beautiful intricate designs. And one night Auntie Daisy brought Nick over to introduce him to her sister. They had just started going out. Well, Nick had brought a bottle of vodka with him and one thing led to another and pretty soon your grandpa got into one of his tirades, ranting about the revolution and how it would smash these old customs and religious rituals once and for all. He got Nick going pretty good too. Daisy tried to get your grandmother to go with her into the other room, let them get on with their drinking and raving. But your grandmother shook her off and stood there looking at your grandpa, arms tight across her body and lips carved shut. He yelled at her to get out and still she stood there, completely expressionless. Staring. And then he stopped yelling and picked up an egg and held her eyes while he hefted the egg in his hand. And still fixing her with his eyes, he threw the egg against the wall. Your grandma didn't even flinch, not once, as one after another he smashed them. Every one. Some of them just exploded into fragments, but some of them hadn't been blown, so green and brown slime ran down the wall. And still she stared at him. Auntie Daisy said she didn't make a sound for all of her work; just mopped up the slime and bits of eggshell with an old rag. But the stench of rotten eggs hung in the house for days. And she never made another Easter egg."

I clear my throat. "Why didn't she go home to her parents?"

My mother hesitates. Swallows. "It's so hard for you to understand. The way things are today. The things we had to do back then, just to stay alive. Dramatic as that sounds, I know." She smiles briefly. "I think she did try to go back. I think that's why we didn't see much of my grandparents when I was growing up. But what could they do? They had other children."

The photos at my elbow are of my great-grandparents, whom I never knew. They are dressed in traditional Ukrainian costume, which I have never seen on any of my relatives. The photos, which we found at the back of the bottom drawer of the sideboard, are in sepia, the colour drained, the intricate patterns of the costumes barely discernible beneath the yellowing and cracking. There is something preternatural about the grimness of their expression. Their stoic bearing. Their impenetrable silence. No wonder my grandmother locked them away.

What I want to say is "What else did he smash?" The night he counted the money and found one dime missing and the smell of orange on his daughter's breath. Is there a point in this story when the crack of eggshell shifts to the crack of bone on bone, when bits of coloured shell are spattered a deeper red? And you, Mother. Are you somewhere in this story, somewhere I cannot follow, hiding with your hands over your ears? There is no frame large enough for this story, no filter that will help me see what, in the end, I do not really want to see. And for this, I want to say, I am sorry.

Some traditions are too strong. I say nothing.

My mother rubs weakly at the smudges under her eyes. I think she would like me to touch her, to hold her, even, but her body looks too brittle. And then I think, perhaps it is I who am too brittle. Too well versed in lessons from a tomato seed, a scrap of warm dough, a bit of rind in a bathrobe pocket. As my mother has said — and probably her mother before her — we do what we must. But I will dare what I can. I reach towards her, take the orange from her hand and section it carefully. I offer one segment to her, place another in my mouth. Then we wait for the flavour to burst upon our tongues.

LIFEGUARD

I'm not all that crazy about small kids. That might seem strange coming from a guy who's a lifeguard at the Bridgeland Community Swimming Pool, but the job gives me free pool time, and I'm training for the city tryouts. Keeping snot-nosed kids from drowning themselves and one another is the only price I have to pay. I made it pretty clear to the kids the first couple days that I wasn't hired as their babysitter or their buddy, and most of them gave me a wide berth after that. Fine by me. I had my own problems that summer.

For one thing, my mom got this great job offer that she couldn't turn down, never mind that this was the year I finally had a chance to make the city team. After four years of being told, You're too small, too thin, not strong enough. Four years of push-ups and sit-ups in the dark in my bedroom after Mom said lights out, of countless lengths in the mornings before school. So I flat out refused to move, and wound up living on my own in Calgary while she and my kid brother lived in Vancouver and kept in touch through weekly phone calls that all went pretty much the same way. Mom would ask how I was doing, and then she'd start to cry and remind me that none of this was her fault, that the Vancouver job paid almost twice as much as her old job and if Dad hadn't run off like he did everything would be just great. Which, when I thought about the time before he took off, made me wonder whether her mind hadn't been cracked by the move. I suppose the good thing about it was that there wasn't much room for me to get too upset, what with her getting upset enough for the both of us. I'd tell her about practice and how my time was really improving and she'd ask if I was remembering to eat right. A few words with the kid bro and that was it for another week.

All of which I was OK with, for the most part. But then, right out of the blue, my dad shows up. After running out on us six years before. I had to look twice to be sure it was him behind the glass in the viewing area, watching me. Watching me watching him. And he doesn't wave or move or even crack a smile. Typical.

I'd been diving before they opened up the pool for the free swim. I get a kick out of doing my dives then, surfacing to catch the kids staring at me with open mouths. I hadn't told anybody, not even my mom, but I wasn't only trying out for the swim team. My real goal was to be on the diving team. High diving. I like everything about it, the swing of my back as I climb the ladder, the metal steps and rungs cold under my feet and hands. I even like the way my stomach falls away when I get to the top and feel the pebbly grain of the platform under my feet. And no matter how many times I dive, my gut always does fall away. Butterflies, my mom calls it. "Butter-flies," she used to sing out into the back seat whenever we hit a big bump driving down into the States on holidays. And my kid brother, who was practically a baby still, would laugh like crazy, with his snorty little laugh that sounds like a sneeze, and try to say, "Butterflies," with her while she reached over from the front seat to tickle his tummy. That was when we were all still a family. I don't remember much about my dad, even though I was old enough to remember. I guess he was just there, hands on the wheel, eyes on the road. I don't really know. I try to picture him doing anything else and that's the best I can do.

I stand at the edge of the platform for a minute, smelling the chlorine and staring into the blue-green square, gathering everything I've got into the centre of my body. A couple of bends at the knee, then up and out, with all the tension in my legs pouring through my chest and straight out the top of my head. Try to hang there forever, stretched out and motionless, then make the body arrow-straight and knife-steady and slice open that pool like it was a melon. There isn't anything like it. When the dive is right it's just you and the air racing away from everything, even from your body.

So anyway, I sploosh out of the pool after a dive and there's a whole bunch of kids jostling in the viewing room. And Dad. We barely lock eyeballs when the doors burst open and all the little buggers cannonball into the pool, yelling fit to break glass. And I'm blowing my whistle and yelling too, so I don't have a lot of time to think about why he's here and what exactly I'm supposed to do about it.

I just get things slightly under control when a finger pokes my arm. I look down and there's Mike. Ever since he first saw me dive, that kid stuck to me like a leech no matter how hard I tried to shake him loose. He was always after me, "How's my crawl doin', Chris?" and "Watch me do the butterfly." So every once in a while, to get some peace, I'd watch him thrash his way around the shallow end of the pool. He was lousy, but no amount of telling him so would get him off my back.

Mike was so scrawny he barely had enough ass to hang swim trunks on, and without his glasses, his eyes were always slightly out of focus, like he was looking at something just beyond you. For all the times I saw him at the pool, and that was almost every day for the whole summer, I don't think I ever saw him swim with anybody — he was always off by himself, puffing and blowing like a baby whale. His mom would drop him off at the gate. She looked a bit like my mom. First time I saw her, I thought for a minute Mom had changed her mind about taking the job in Vancouver. After his mom left, Mike spent all his time paddling in the shallow end. And bugging me. Like I didn't have better things to do with my time.

So I'm scanning the viewing room to see if my dad's still there, only my eyes keep getting snagged on one of the babes that hang out at the pool in a bathing suit that's a clear signal they don't come for the swimming, and she looks away and laughs with her friends and I'm hoping she was watching when I made that dive. I hadn't taken my eyes off the pool for more than a few minutes but all of a sudden I see Mike splashing around in the deep end. So I'm in the pool like a flash, hauling him to the surface and throwing him onto the edge like a dead mackerel. "You dumb little shit! What do you think you're doing down this end of the pool? You could've drowned!"

He stands there streaming with water and this weird, shining kind of look.

"Wow! That is so cool!"

I glance over to the viewing area. No sign of my dad, and the girls have moved on too.

I poke Mike in the chest, hard. "Cut the crap, man. What the hell were you doing down in the deep end?"

"You gotta try it, Chris."

"Try what?" The little snot has gone off the deep end in more ways than one.

"Look, I'll show you." And he starts off back to where I've just finished hauling him out. Some people you have to hit over the head with a sledgehammer. I yank him back by the arm.

"Haven't you heard a word I've been saying? You're not allowed down there unless you can swim a length."

"Why should I have to swim a length?" the kid asks. "Anybody knows that even if you fall in in the middle of the pool, the most you'd have to swim is half a width."

"Yeah, well, for you that'd still be pushing it."

"If I swim the width will you let me show you?"

"Show me what?"

He answered with the slow patience you'd treat someone with who wasn't wrapped too tight. "If I have to show you, I can't tell you, can I?" And then before I can say anything, in he dives — into the deep end again, couldn't prove his point in the shallow end, not Mike. Well, he's moving like an egg-beater, churning up the water and looking like he'll go down any minute. But I have to admit that he's made it when he comes back up to me.

"Now watch," he says, like he's going to open me up to some kind of miracle.

What I see convinces me that the little squirt is definitely a little bent. He crouches down at the edge of the pool and rolls himself up into a ball, then slowly tips himself off the edge backwards, gradually unfolding as he sinks deeper and deeper into the water. I keep waiting for some sort of trick, but all he does is a limp deadman's float underneath the surface of the water, not moving, only wafting like a fleshy seaweed. The longer he stays there the more nervous I get, and I'm just thinking I'm going to have to go in after him a second time when he slowly rises to the surface, bursting through near the ladder. He comes running up to me with the same goofy expression, like a pup that figures it's been really clever. "Did you see, Chris? Did you see?"

"See *what*?"

He stares at me like *I'm* the moron.

"It's like ... like falling into a ... a cloud, and it ..." I tap my forehead with one finger and draw circles in the air. Mike's voice fizzles. "I guess you have to do it yourself to figure it out." He tugs at my finger. "Why don't you try it, Chris? It feels really neat."

"I have to get back to work, kid. I can't stand around all day listening to weirdos." I start to walk away. But he's a persistent guy and you've got to admit he doesn't take an insult. He tags along, saying, "Yeah, but you will try it, won't you, Chris?"

"Yeah, yeah, sure, kid." I keep walking.

That Sunday the usual phone call took an unusual turn.

"Dad came by the pool last week."

"How on earth did he find you? After six years!" Mom clamps down on this outburst and there's a long, murky pause; then she says, too carefully, "What did you two talk about?"

"We didn't. He just stood there. He watched me practise and then he left."

"If that isn't exactly like him, to wait for you to make the ..." She reins in her voice hard, and takes a minute before going on. "What do you think you'll do about it?"

"I don't know. He left."

"He'll be back." Her voice is too neutral, gives nothing away, and I feel like I'm straining to see her face, to find out what she thinks I should do, but all I can see is the blank wall of the kitchen.

"Shit, Mom, I don't know."

"Don't swear, Chris," but she says it automatically, not like she's mad. "Honey, I don't know either. You have to do what's best for you."

Thanks a lot, I think. All the times she couldn't keep her nose out of my business, telling me what to do, and for the first time in ages, when I'd actually like at least a hint, now I'm grown up enough to decide for myself.

"Yeah, well. I guess I'll let you know."

"OK, dear." Another pause and then, almost like a question, "I love you."

"I know, Mom. I know."

"Do you want to talk to your brother?"

"Naw, I'll catch him next time. I gotta go."

She was right of course. He came back. Every few days I'd look up from the water and see him behind the glass. He never came beyond it and I never waved or motioned in any way. And I knew that he was leaving it up to me to decide. The asshole, I thought. Serve him right if one of these days I walk up to that viewing room, shove open the door and pop him one right in the mouth. Tell him exactly what I've been thinking of him in the years he's been gone. I had a lot of fantasies like that, and they got my blood boiling pretty good, but the ones that made me even madder were the ones that snuck in when I was off my guard, the ones where he looked at me and half smiled, a little nervous, and said he was sorry for everything.

"So how does he look?" Mom asked on one of my calls.

Old, I think. Seeing not only the greying hair that dipped across his forehead, but the lines around the eyes and mouth, deep enough to see even through glass. "He looks OK, I guess." For a minute I think, why not tell the truth, dummy?

You don't have to protect him. And then I realize it's not him I'm protecting. I remember what it was like when he was around. Mom talking all the time, especially towards the end. Dad barely talking at all. Me shunted between the two of them, Mom pushing Dad to take me to the park, then pulling me aside and asking me what he said, whether he left me alone there. It was almost a relief when he took off. Almost but not quite. The first couple years I used to see him everywhere, only it was never him. It was so typical that he'd finally show up once I got used to the fact that he was gone. And that thought would get me boiling all over again.

Mike was at the pool almost every day, not swimming, just playing his strange little game. Every so often he'd bug me to watch him, but my temper was not the best and usually I told him to buzz off. I was spending every spare minute at the pool, even helping to clean up after the last Belly-Burner Aquacise class ended at eleven. I'd come back early in the morning and spend hours swimming lengths, paring precious seconds off my time. At the end of one of these sessions I could barely stand. I pushed myself with my diving too, leaping harder, trying to go higher, come down faster, cleaner, deeper. One day, Keith, one of the older lifeguards who also did some diving yelled at me to get out of the pool and then dragged me into the office, wet and shivering. Didn't even give me time to get my towel. He glared at me and plugged in a video of the Olympic Games a few years back. A Russian diver miscalculated his dive and hit the platform on his way down. The moment of impact didn't look like anything much; he barely glanced off the edge, nothing dramatic at all. But you could tell he was in trouble the minute he hit. His body. It just dropped, like there was no one inside it any more. And then the water bloomed red from the bottom of the pool. I felt sick. Keith switched off the VCR. "I don't know what you're thinking about out there, kid," he said, "but it isn't diving. And if you're not thinking about diving, stay the hell off the platform."

I barely opened my mouth to say something when he stared me down and said, "I don't want to hear it. Stop assing around out there or I'll have you banned from this pool."

It's hard to try for righteous indignation when you're practically naked and shaking with cold and anger, so I slammed out of the office, and straight into Mike.

"Hi, Chris. You OK? Did he ream you out?"

I swear, I tried to keep walking and not talk to him, but he grabbed my hand and something snapped. I turned around with my fist raised, like I was going to smack him, and yelled straight into his nerdy face, "Leave me the hell alone, you little geek. Just fuck off and leave me alone!" I stomped off to the changing rooms without even a glance at the viewing area. Just my luck my dad'd be there in time to see me practically cream some kid a quarter my size. Well, I didn't want to know about it, thank you very much.

So naturally, when Mike stopped coming to the pool, I figured it had to be because I'd yelled at him. I felt pretty bad but, honestly, he was such a pain in the neck, and I figured he'd get over it. Then one day I overheard a couple of parents talking while their kids were getting showered. Talking about Mike's family, in that hush-hush, greedy voice people use when they go over gory details. Mike and his parents had been driving up to Saskatchewan to see some relatives. Just out of Drumheller they'd been hit head-on by a kid out joyriding, playing chicken with another guy. Asshole pulled out to pass on a curve and hit Mike's family doing about a hundred klicks. His buddy didn't even stop, but a Greyhound bus driver saw the whole thing and radioed the police. When they got there Mike's mom was squashed like an accordion under the dashboard, and his dad was walking in big crazy circles all over the road, muttering to himself in gibberish and flapping his arms like a chicken. Mike had crawled into the corner farthest from his mom, in the back seat, and was staring from behind his shattered glasses, from one parent to the other, folded in on himself like a tight, hard ball.

Well, you can imagine what a shit I felt then. The pool is right near the hospital they had Mike at, so I went over to see him after work. I talked to a nurse there, and she filled me in on the rest of the story. Mike's mom was killed on impact; his dad took a few days more to go. They did a whole bunch of tests on Mike, and apart from some cuts and a big bruise on his forehead he was OK. Physically.

Since they'd brought him in he hadn't said a word or looked like he could hear anyone. They couldn't even tell if he knew his parents were dead. He didn't move, didn't speak, barely blinked. There wasn't a friend or a relative who could take him — he had to be dressed and changed like a baby — so they were sending him to a Home a few blocks away.

I went up to his room and it was spooky the way he just sat there, staring at nothing. He didn't even look at me. I felt funny trying to talk to him, so I only stayed a few minutes that day. But the Home was even closer to the pool than the hospital, so I got into the habit of dropping in on him every couple of days. He got on pretty well there. In a few weeks he was walking again, and going to the toilet himself. But nobody could get a peep out of him. I almost gave up going, but I couldn't get him out of my head, he looked so scrawny and small behind his glasses. And apart from feeling sorry for the guy, I found out it's actually pretty cool talking to somebody who can't talk back. Easier to open up when the person doesn't say anything stupid to shut you back down again. Or when they don't have a stake in what's on your mind. It got so I'd talk to Mike a lot, and I even looked forward to it.

Things went on this way for most of the summer. The last week in August were my tryouts. The swimming one went great. All those lengths stood me in good stead and I was solidly in the middle range for the team. But my diving tryout was a total bomb. I got to the edge of the platform and nothing went the way it usually does. No butterflies, no rush from the smell of chlorine. The pool looked too close, too real, my legs and arms felt too big, gangly, in the way. And what clinched it was my dad. There again, behind the viewing glass. No smile, no wave. You bastard, I thought, I'll show you, and I flung myself into my dive like a knife-thrower. It was a disaster. No hang-time, in fact I felt so rushed I barely had time to straighten out and avoid the total humiliation, not to mention pain, of a belly-flop. I knew as soon as I got out of the water that I'd blown it. I wanted to ask for a second chance, but I was afraid I'd start blubbering all over the place if I opened my mouth, so I had to just stand there tight-lipped, my chest clenched like a fist, while the coach told me really nicely that I was trying too hard, I had to learn to let go and let the dive take me with it. I couldn't even thank her when she suggested I come to some training sessions she was giving at the Y. By the time I headed for the showers my dad was gone.

I didn't go see Mike for five days after that. I showed up for work and went home and that was about it. My dad didn't show up either. I was watching for him. Then the nurse called me. She'd gotten my name from the sign-in sheet and looked up my number in the phone book. Just wanted to know how I was doing, she said, but I knew she wanted to know why I'd suddenly stopped visiting. Christ, I thought, even when he can't speak the kid finds a way to hassle me. But I told her I'd be by the next day.

I stopped at the door of his room, and watched him for a minute, breathing that pale, washed-out smell you get in hospitals. Lying in that big white square of a bed he looked like he had been swallowed whole. The fist in my chest squeezed tighter and I thought, it's too much, I can't do it. But I pasted a big smile on my face, walked to the side of the bed and sat down.

"Hey, Mikey," I said.

He looked at me. Turned his head and looked at me. And when I figured out he really was in there somewhere, I couldn't help it, I started to cry. And I told him about the tryouts and my dad and how crappy it was, what with my mom being no help at all and me not knowing whether I wanted to talk to him or kill him. And the whole time I was thinking, good going, Chris, the kid just lost both his parents and may never get a chance at a normal life, and you're busy telling him all your pissant little problems, but I just couldn't help it.

Finally I scrubbed my face and said, "Sorry, kid. Guess you've got problems of your own, eh?" But he was gone again, not a flicker in his eyes, staring beyond me. "Well, at least I still have my day job. They've asked me to teach swimming a couple nights a week. Most of the kids are worse swimmers than you, and boy, is that saying something." Still nothing. And suddenly it became the most important thing in the world to get him to look at me again. "Listen, Mikey, they're putting in a whirlpool for sports injury therapy. Looks pretty neat. Why don't you come to the pool sometime? Would you like that?"

He touched my face with one finger.

Well, I was like a crazy man, running up to the nurse all excited, shouting my head off. And she was just as bad. So that was how he started coming to the pool again, only this time a volunteer attendant brought him. The guy would sit Mike in the shallow end and kind of play with him, splashing him lightly with water, letting him walk around. Mike seemed to be quite happy just to sit or paddle. He was tired and old-looking, too feeble to resist when the attendant steered him away from the deep end. I began to think that this might be the best he'd ever do.

Then one day, while the attendant is talking to one of the girls in the new Jacuzzi, I see Mike head for the deep end, walking close to the edge, jerkily, like he's on automatic pilot. The deep end is near the Jacuzzi and I figure it's only a matter of moments before the volunteer sees what the kid's up to and hauls him away, so I casually wander over to the whirl-pool and block his view. All the time I'm watching Mike out of the corner of my eye and trying to convince myself that if he starts to get into trouble I can get him out of it, but I'm still pretty nervous. How the hell do I really know why he's off to that end of the pool, anyway? But another part of me, lower down, is drumming out this message over and over, telling him to go for it, go for it, and I don't even know what I mean. Well, Mike gets to the deep end and, sure enough, the attend-ant looks over my shoulder and freaks. He leaps out of the whirlpool as Mike crouches down, but I hold him back by one arm. "Leave him alone, man."

"Are you crazy?" he says. "You're gonna get me fired."

"Fuck off," I say, eyes glued to the kid.

Mike tips himself backwards into the pool.

"Jesus H. Christ!" yells the volunteer and hurls himself

towards the pool, only to come smack up against me. I'm ready to punch him out if he takes one more step towards that kid, so help me God. Mike is floating like a dead man, loose and motionless beneath the water. My heart is thrashing the inside of my chest when I think of what could be happening if I'm wrong. The attendant is staring at me like I'm a murderer, and I'm grunting with the strain of holding him back when suddenly I realize I haven't been keeping track of my breathing. I don't know how long he's been in there.

Maybe this is what he intended all along. Maybe he figured he could trust me to let him go.

Maybe he's two steps above vegetable and whatever's left of him is somewhere in there screaming for help.

"MIKEY!" I yell at the pool. But I don't move one step closer.

The attendant is practically crying, and a ragged group is forming behind us, trying to figure out what's happening, what we're staring at.

Mike's arms and legs start to move. He looks like he's feeling his way through some invisible tunnel, then he bursts through into the open air, climbs out of the pool and walks back to the same spot, more confidently, almost eagerly. He tips himself backwards again, eyes closed.

My hands are still digging into the attendant's arms — he'll have a hell of a bruise, and I think I've strained a muscle in my wrist. We breathe in our first wild gulps, and stand there panting for a few seconds after I let him go. "See," I say while he rubs the red spots, "it's just his game. He's OK. I'll watch him." We dance around a little, 'cause I've wounded the guy's pride, but basically he's cool.

I turn away to check the rest of the pool, and there's my dad in the viewing room. He's seen the whole thing. I can tell because his face is twisted like he's in pain, and he looks like he's ready to step through the glass like it's nothing but air. Our eyes lock, and his hands rise to the glass and press against it, fingers spread wide open. And it's like what he's feeling is so strong it pulls my hand towards it all by itself. But that's where it ends. Every muscle in my body aches. I need to sit down, rub my wrists. I need. And all he does is stand there.

I still spend a lot of time at the pool. My dad comes by,

but not so often, and I find myself looking for him less and less. When he does show, I don't make a move to go talk to him. I figure there are some things you have to work out on your own. Maybe he will, maybe he won't. Maybe he'll just disappear again. But that's up to him. In the meantime, I have things to get on with. My diving lessons at the Y. And Mike. Like I promised, I watch him, every day, while he tips himself into the depths of that big fluffy cloud or living pool or hands of God or whatever his bent little brain thinks is there. Most days he doesn't give any sign that he knows I'm here. But I know I am, and I guess that's what matters. And I'll tell you something else. Every time he breaks water it's like some kind of underwater flower bursting into the sunlight, and I swear I can feel the touch of something warm on my face.

MINOR ALTERATIONS

Marnie sits on the cold vinyl bench, cold sneaking through her jeans, climbing her spine to the bare breasts bumping against the pale blue paper gown. The slick of sweat that is always between her breasts and ribcage itches. She hopes he won't have to pick up her breasts and touch the sticky spot. She hopes this can be decided quickly. If it could be done in the office while she waited, she would do it immediately.

The chart on the other side of the closed door rustles. A rapid knock-knock; the handle turns.

His coat is pristine over black trouser legs that poke out at knee level. His leather shoes squeak. He closes the door precisely, smiles beneath greying eyebrows.

"I assume my receptionist explained that this is just a preliminary visit to give you an idea of what to expect," he says, smiling with even white teeth.

"Yes," Marnie says. She wonders if he has had his teeth straightened. A plastic surgeon has to look good. A smile glimmers within her but doesn't quite make it to her face. She has a trick for just this kind of situation. She can do it with her eyes open, her body apparently relaxed while inside herself she is spinning away from her skin, smaller and smaller, until she peeks out from behind a rib, safe from the hands that will explore her surface.

"Good." He is at the sink, washing his hands. Squeak of lather on skin. His hands are very pale. She hopes they will not be cold.

"All right then," he says in a smooth voice. "Let's have a look." And he peels back the gown, whisper of paper on skin, cool air a breath behind. Gooseflesh springs up around her nipples.

He probes each breast, fingers sinking into the heavy, blue-veined globes. "Mmm, no problem there," he says. "What size were you thinking about?" His hand rests just under the breast, as though weighing it.

Marnie forces herself not to pull away. His hand is warm and that seems more repulsive to her now than the cold she dreaded. Her mind wheels. Size? Does he want inches? God in heaven, will he pull out a chart and convert to metric? Deep below her surface, a rumble.

When she hesitates, the doctor says, "You seem quite young to be taking this kind of step. However, I assume you've thought about it a good deal?"

She has been trying to do anything but. It was Robert's idea that she look into getting a breast reduction. One night he traced with his finger the permanent bruises on her shoulders, caused by her bra straps, and said it couldn't be healthy, that much weight, could it? And so Marnie looked up plastic surgeons in the Yellow Pages and phoned. The surgeon was booked solid and couldn't fit her in for a month, and for almost that whole month she managed not to think about it at all. Instead she found herself going back in her mind to the Mykonos Restaurant and Lounge. Crash of dishes and swearing of cooks in the kitchen, steamy dishwasher going full blast, garlic and feta and tomato strong in the nose and sly sips of retsina harsh on the tongue — all the details sunk low in her memory, labelled *Life before Robert*. Before everything, really.

"Waitress, over here!"

The lounge was packed and she was run off her high-heeled feet. When she'd first started the job she had worn brown loafers, pleated wool skirts, and blazers or loose-fitting sweaters. The kind of clothes her mother had always said stopped her from looking all bust. After a couple of days Zaros had taken her aside in the coat-check room and said, Look kid, it's a restaurant, not an office, why not get yourself some sexier clothes and shoes and raise your liquor sales? That's where the money is, liquor sales, and the tips too, he'd added, tapping her ass lightly with a coat hanger. So she had bought a black sweater with rhinestone buttons, and a purple skirt that was tight over the hips but flared out to just above knee level, and she thought she looked pretty good. Not slender, never that. But good in a fleshy sort of way. If you liked curves she was passable.

"Yes sir, is everything all right?"

He was with his wife; at least, Marnie assumed the woman was his wife. He'd ordered for both of them — steak, baked potato, salad with house dressing. Maybe the steak wasn't cooked the way he liked it — medium rare, he'd said. She could see brown and red juices leaking into the baked potato, but didn't know if that meant it was medium rare or not. Marnie liked her meat cooked.

"Sir?"

"You know," he said with a smile, "I've been watching you for some time, and I have to say, you must have awfully big feet."

"Excuse me?"

"I said you must have awfully big feet." Marnie glanced at his wife for some kind of clue, but the woman's eyes were fixed on her plate as she searched for a crouton beneath layers of lettuce. The man's eyes were riveted to her rhinestone buttons, and Marnie had to make an effort not to move her hands to her breasts. She stared dumbly at him, not sure what to do. People at other tables were watching, and she probably had an order up in the kitchen. Why wouldn't he just get to the point? His wife was scraping up creamy house dressing with her fork. The man's eyes were still at her chest as he said with the same friendly smile, "I can't figure out how it is you don't fall right over."

Marnie inhales deeply.

"Yes, I've thought about it," she says.

"Good. Well, what I always do is show the patient where the scars will be and then send you home to reflect." He pulls out a ballpoint pen, pushes one breast up against Marnie's upper chest to make things a bit easier, then pulls the skin around her nipple taut between his thumb and forefinger. Her skin snags the nib as he draws a circle round the nipple. It tickles, and sends a shiver to her groin. She blushes, tries not to squirm. He pushes the breast up still farther and draws a line straight down from the nipple along the curve of the breast to the ribcage. But when he tries to draw a semicircle along the lower curve of the breast, his pen slides over the sweat there, refuses to leave a mark. Marnie's cheeks burn as he flops the breast down, goes over to the sink and comes back with a tissue. He lifts the breast again, wipes away the faint trace of sweat, then goes back to his task. Marnie stares over the top of his head at the certificates on the wall. Tries to lose focus. The trick isn't working. She keeps trying to retreat, but he keeps calling her back.

She never did say anything to the man in the restaurant. Just walked away. She thinks now, though she has remembered and restructured the scene so many times she can't be sure, that she may have cast the woman one long look of pity before turning her back. Funny. To put it all on the woman like that.

She didn't even quit the restaurant. The man wasn't a regular and, as it turned out, he never came back, so there was no point in making a fuss, though she did invest in a bra that encased and controlled her breasts with underwires and thick straps, an ugly contraption with lace trim. A few weeks later she met Robert. He was dining alone. She was drawn to him from the moment she took his drink order, the touch of grey at his temples, the neat press of his suit, the vulnerability of a few sparse hairs along his slightly receding hairline. Before carrying his martini to the table she straightened her sweater, smoothed down her skirt, sucked in her tummy muscles and held them tight. Under those cool grey eyes she felt the rhinestone buttons a shade large, the shade of purple a touch gaudy.

He took an appreciative swallow of martini, rolling it round his tongue, then carefully unfolded his napkin while she waited for his food order. She made it her business to give him perfect service, alert to the exact level of wine in his glass, the moment his knife and fork lay parallel across his plate. And as he dropped his credit card lightly onto the bill tray he said, "Are you free for a drink after work?"

"I really shouldn't."

He smiled. "I'll pick you up at midnight."

She tumbled into bed with him that same night, and he tended to her body with the same care and precision she had observed in his handling of his napkin and cutlery, his fingers etching intricate patterns of desire on her skin. They stayed in bed three days. "Don't leave," he said. "Phone in sick," and so she did, Robert nibbling at her ear, teasing her nipples with his fingertips, while she tried to convince Zaros she had the flu. Robert wouldn't even let her go out for groceries, and they ate their way through his refrigerator, bringing back to the bed cheese and crackers, fruit and milk or wine, so as not to be too long absent from the mingling of their moist scents in the sheets and pillows. At one point when she got up to go to the bathroom he held her hand, pulling her back, and cried, "That's *my* body, bring it back here," and she laughed and laughed and loved him from that moment. When he finally let her go she stood before her reflection in the mirror, tousled hair, eyes slightly bruised with lack of sleep, mouth swollen with kisses. For the first time she thought, "I am beautiful." And she ran her hands over the breasts he had kissed, the hips he had strained against, cherishing this body that he had cherished until the cold defeated her and she scurried back to bed. Shivering, she slid beside him and tried to nuzzle in close, but he held her away from him so that he could look at her. With strong hands he scooped her hair up on either side of her face, cradling her skull. "You have such beautiful hair," he murmured, the strands tumbling between his knuckles. "Look at all these gold highlights. You really should cut it to show them off more, you know."

She lost her job because Zaros phoned her apartment to find out how she was doing and her roommate hadn't seen her for three days. But she didn't care. She packed up her things, leaving most of her clothes behind on Robert's suggestion. He would buy all she needed. And she revelled in it. Make me new, Robert. Mould me, shape me. Make me yours. Lovely. Loved.

"Now, these marks are where you'd have scars," the doctor says, flicking the nib of the ballpoint back into the barrel. "First we make an incision round here and remove the nipple, then make another down the midsection of the breast and along the bottom, and kind of fold the skin over." His fingers trace the lines on her skin. "Do you sew? My wife does; says it reminds her of making a dart, just tucking in the excess material" — he pinches together a fold of her skin — "like so. Quite simple, really." He releases her skin and it relaxes into its original contours.

"What about ... pain?"

"Well, that's a problematic question since people seem to experience pain at different levels. Most of the women I've seen seem to feel the end results are worth the discomfort." He clips the pen to his white coat pocket, eyes lowered to this task, so that Marnie can't see his expression when he continues. "Pain is a relative thing, really."

From the first, Marnie loved Robert's drive for perfection, the way he pinched the skin at his taut belly and grimaced if he could capture more than a quarter of an inch, added an extra twenty sit-ups to his nightly routine. He had told her about how his father had died young, how his mother, back in England, wrote only about her ailments, one thing after another, some real, some imagined. He was not going to end up like either one of them, and she admired that will, that strength of purpose. If you see something wrong, change it. She would lie in bed and watch him exercise, delighting in the ripple of stomach and chest muscles. "Why not join me?" he asked once, and she chuckled, whipping back the sheets in invitation. "Why bother when I can get all the exercise I need lying down?"

She began to come across self-improvement books he left lying around the bathroom, bedroom, kitchen, splayed open at chapters on diet and exercise, self-esteem. At first she just closed them and stacked them neatly on his side of the bed. But one day she flipped through a book called *The Psychology of Winning*, the chapter on how to see yourself as you really are. Strip completely, and put a paper bag over your head, with holes cut so you can see out; then examine yourself from every angle. The author's theory was that when you look in the mirror every day you focus on your friendly, familiar face and can ignore the flab, the flaws, the wrinkles. Cut off that face, blot it out, and you see the headless body of a stranger.

She got as far as cutting the holes in the paper bag and standing naked to the side of the bedroom mirror. Terrified to put the bag over her head. Suppose she looked and the flaws were endless? The whole thing was crazy, she decided, as she ripped the bag into small pieces and shoved them to the bottom of the garbage can.

That night, while Robert read a book on risk communication, she continued with *The Psychology of Winning*, which told her that men should maintain their optimum body weight at about 170 pounds. And women theirs at about 115. Oh come on, she thought. It reminded her of a *National Geographic* special she'd seen on sea lions, with great galumphing jowly males pushing around sleek little lionesses half their size. She turned to share this joke with Robert but thought better of it. Underneath the bedclothes she pinched the skin at her waist.

Marnie started jogging, breasts bouncing painfully. She pushed herself to keep up with Robert, even though he tried to stop her. "You have to start slow, Marnie. Going at it this hard could hurt you. Why not turn back?" "I'm fine," she said, half doubled over from a stitch in her side. "No pain, no gain, right?"

She listened with painful acuity to his every word, searching for clues to his desires. When he said that he liked her in mauve, she had her colours done to find her exact shade of mauve, head small above a white sheet, swatches of material laid against this pure canvas. She had her hair streaked to highlight it even more, sitting with a plastic mesh cap over her head while the hairdresser yanked strands through with a tiny metal hook. Robert loved her, she knew that he loved her, for who she was. She would just make sure that she was as much who she was as she could get. And so, of course, when he mentioned the bra-strap bruises and traced them with his finger, she knew what he was hinting at. He didn't have to say another word.

The doctor walks to a cabinet in one corner of the room and pulls out a piece of paper from a file. "This is the waiver you'll have to sign if you decide to go ahead with the procedure." He has not once called it surgery. "It tells you the things that could go wrong."

Marnie holds the paper between numb fingers. "Can you give me a rough idea...?"

"Well, for example, with all cases involving a general anaesthetic, there's some risk. That's laid out here." He points at the paper, then runs his finger down a few sentences. "Here you'll see that, even though we try our best, we can't always guarantee that both breasts will be exactly the same size. And of course, because we actually remove the nipple and then reattach it, there can be, in rare cases, some problems with blood supply. Occasionally, very occasionally, the nipple doesn't get the proper blood supply, and in that case reattachment fails to take place." He clears his throat. "What I mean is, the nipple could detach itself. Permanently." For the first time he looks directly into Marnie's eyes, and says, quite kindly, really, "I'm sorry to be so blunt, but you do have to know all these things before you decide to go ahead."

The day Marnie turned fifteen, her parents gave her a beauty book by Vidal and Beverly Sassoon and then took her shopping. They were having coffee in the mall when the sign caught her father's eye: *Hair removal, European wax expert.*

"Why not check it out?" he said to Marnie.

"Oh, I don't know, Dad." She had always thought he couldn't see the hairs on her chin. Maybe he had just avoided saying anything to spare her feelings.

"No, seriously, Marnie," her mother said, squinting at the finer print under the sign, "why not? You could probably get everything done. Sideburns, chin, even your upper lip. You have a little bit of a moustache, you know."

Marnie's hand went to her chin. She tried to keep the hairs controlled with tweezers, but every now and then she missed some.

Her face flamed. She felt as embarrassed as she had the time her father had slammed down his knife and fork on the dinner table halfway through supper and told her to get a better bra because she was bouncing so much she was making him dizzy. Or the time he'd told her to stop using his washcloth when she took a shower because she was leaving pubic hairs in it. But Marnie never used a washcloth, only her hands. Not that she said that to her father.

"She's just shy, aren't you, dear?" her mother said. "You go on up to the Safeway, Dad, and I'll go in with her. We'll meet you when we're done. Come on, Marnie. At least we can check the prices. Maybe they could even take you now."

As her mother led her into the salon, Marnie began to feel hopeful that one problem at least could be solved. Specifically, that when she went out with her boyfriend, one of his moron friends always kidded her about having more of a moustache than Darin did.

"Oh, I can see exactly what you mean," the receptionist said, holding Marnie's face in her hand and turning it this way and that. "Don't you worry about a thing." Her touch so candid, so accepting, a cool promise of smooth and glowing skin. "We can have you fixed up in no time."

"What exactly is involved in the procedure?" Marnie's mother asked.

"It's quite simple, really." The receptionist smiled. "We spread melted wax over the area, let it cool slightly and then pull it off and, voilà, the hair comes with it."

"See, Marnie?" her mother said. "Simple."

And in no time Marnie was in the chair, with the petite blonde waxer showing her mother the routine. The electrically heated bowl of wax, a sickly yellow colour; the wooden palette knife.

The hot wax on her lower jaw and chin brought tears to Marnie's eyes. She saw herself a blur in the mirror, ugly yellow splotches over her face one minute; a tearing wrench, and the yellow splotches flushed an angry red. "Darn," the waxer said. "Missed some, we'll have to try again. How are you doing? OK?"

Of course I'm not OK, Marnie wanted to yell. You just yanked off half my face with the first try and now you want to pour molten wax on what's left. But she couldn't say anything, not with her mother standing over her. She had asked if she could watch.

"OK," Marnie said.

"Sometimes we have to go over the area up to four times to get all the hairs," the waxer said, scooping up a blob of yellow wax.

Marnie's tears edged up over the rim of her eyes, leaked back into her hairline.

The next day Marnie stared at her face in the mirror and spread the cooling lotion the waxer had given her over the sullen red patches on her upper lip, her cheeks, her chin. Tiny white pimples springing up over the red patches.

How was she supposed to go to school? She looked like a clown. She glared at the blotch in the mirror, glared while the figure shrank smaller and smaller, glared until it became a pinprick in the glass and vanished.

This trick became very helpful later, when her father discovered a new depilatory tool, an over-the-counter electrolysis machine that zapped the hair at the root and supposedly killed it forever. Marnie would lie down on the couch while either her father or her mother laboured over her, lips pursed in concentration, like sculptors pursuing their image of perfection, zapping her chin and upper lip with tiny electric shocks until their hands got tired. After a while, Marnie got so good at leaving her body that she didn't feel the shocks at all.

"Well, I think that about covers everything," the doctor says. "You haven't said much, but perhaps you need to go home and think it all through." He hesitates, glances at her left hand. "You're not married?"

"No, not exactly. There is someone, though. Someone serious."

He looks relieved. "Oh, well that's all right then. You go home and talk it over with him. For most women the scarring fades with time, and sometimes vitamin E helps. Still, he'll have to live with it too."

"Yes, I suppose he will."

After he leaves, Marnie dresses, then stands in front of the small mirror in profile. She presses her hands down on her breasts, flattening them, trying to imagine how she'll look. How her clothes will hang. Whether the contours of her belly will be more noticeable once the upper curves are gone. Whether she will ever make love with the lights on again.

When Marnie gets home there is a message on the phone machine from Robert. She phones his business number and he answers on the first ring.

"How'd it go?" he asks.

"Fine, Robert, just fine." A buzz on the line makes it difficult to hear what he's saying.

"Well, what did he say? How did he seem?"

"Oh, he said it would be perfectly straightforward, really."

Marnie holds the phone slightly away from her ear, but the buzzing only gets louder.

"You know you don't have to decide right away, it's a big step."

She twists the phone in her hand, winds the cord round her finger. Coil after coil of black rubber twining round her finger. The connection is appalling, the crackle threatening to become a roar. "I have to go now, Robert."

"Wait a minute, Marnie," Robert calls. "I wanted to know ... are you all right? I mean ... how do you feel?"

Marnie slams the phone down and stands by the desk holding her head. Feel. That's a joke.

In the master bathroom she strips off sweater and bra, stands in front of the mirror and sees herself as if for the first time. Stares at the blue lines round her nipples, under her breasts, these lumps of flesh that hang halfway to her waist, stuck onto her without her consent at age thirteen, not really her at all. "They're so beautiful," Darin had said to her once, his hand under her sweater, then caught himself. "I mean, you. You're so beautiful." After they broke up she found out he and his friends had been calling her Mammary Smith behind her back.

Her breasts loom in the mirror, large white circles and within them smaller brown ones rimmed with blue. They look enormous, threaten to fill the entire glass square. She looks like a dressmaker's dummy. And for some reason that makes her think of those horrible, horrible jokes: What do you call a man with no arms or legs hanging on a wall? Art.

With her pointer finger she traces each line, fingernail cool on hot skin, then runs her finger along breastbone and neck to her chin. The faintest stubble of hairs returning. She grips one lone hair that escaped the waxing and yanks. Hard. Depilation. Mammoplasty.

A nip here, a tuck there. A whittling away.

What has she been doing?

Wrenching on the taps, she blasts hot water into the sink, lathers up her hand and a washcloth and scrubs and scrubs at the lines. Imagines one of the nipples popping off and bouncing down the drain. She bites back a laugh.

What do you call a woman with no nipples? Barbie?

Panting, she examines the breasts she has rubbed red and raw. Nothing. The lines haven't faded at all. She can't decide whether they look like they are severing her into chunks or whether they are the only things keeping her from flying apart.

When is a breast not a breast?

Half naked, Marnie walks uncaring past the open windows, soapy water dripping from her breasts onto her jeans, onto the hardwood floor.

What do you call two stick men with a blob between them? Two men walking a breast. Get it?

She fishes in the writing desk in the kitchen till she finds a red felt pen with a wide nib.

Eyes fixed on her reflection in the kitchen window, she slowly and methodically draws over every blue line, pen digging into her skin, scoring the flesh over and over, until she looks as though she is dripping blood.

What do you call a woman with a paper bag over her head? Darling?

She digs deeper, grinding into the skin with the felt tip, until she is sure some of the dye is stained with her own blood. Until she feels pain.

This is a start.

When is a breast not a breast? When it's a blueprint.

Gripping the uncapped pen in her fist, she sits at the kitchen table. The kitchen is cool; she is shivering and goosefleshed. But she shouldn't have to stand it for long. Robert will be worried. He'll be home soon. And before he can even open his mouth or his arms she will share with him the biggest joke of all. She will say, Knock knock, Robert.

Just so she can hear him say, Who's there?

THE QUICK

Baba's at it again. Chewing. She has nibbled her fingernails till they lie red and ridged beneath bumps of skin. She gnaws for an elusive piece of cuticle, chews that too, strips it back, tearing surface skin with it — red half-moons of raw skin against white half-moons of what little healthy nail remains. She mines for cuticle from the side of the nail, releases a tiny red stream, and then Baba sucks absently till the bleeding stops.

"Have they phoned yet?" she mouths around one wounded finger.

"No, Baba."

She is working on a hangnail now. I think she tries to see how far she can snake the strip of skin down her finger before it snaps.

"Please, Baba" — I pull her fingers from her mouth, threads of saliva calling them back. She, they, so ugly — wrinkled fingers in a sunken mouth. "Please don't." But as soon as I turn away she's back at it, nibbling, sucking.

"Did you visit him today?" She wobbles one finger at the air, waving away pain.

"No, Baba, not yet."

Lately she's been worse. She has eczema at the hairline, small outcrops of flaky skin spread between fine white hairs. "Nerves or old age," the doctor says with a shrug, "who can say?" Her fingers probe among the hairs as if tilling barren soil, then travel to her mouth, powdered with loose skin. She tastes, samples, licks. Now the eczema has spread to her fingers, and she alternates between scalp and hand, peeling away tiny parchments, translucent and brittle. Until I find myself plucking at my own hairline, checking my fingers for scaly patches.

The living room is exactly as it has been for all the years I can remember: a purple afghan protecting the couch, some Ukrainian eggs in a dish on the cabinet, a basket of neatly rolled skeins of wool ready for the next afghan or sweater. Baba and Dido have lived here forty years. I once told Baba that Canadians move on average every five years. It's not just me, I was saying beneath the words, flying in on ever briefer visits from Saskatoon, then Winnipeg, then Toronto. It's the whole damn country. A nation of transients. No one stays put any more. "Every five years? Such nonsense," she said, and gave me one of her looks. I writhed under it at the time, adult though I was. Now her eyes glance off the walls, the afghans, the bits of coloured wool, and never settle anywhere, least of all on me.

I am running out of time. My leave lasts only until the spring and I was lucky to get that much. "I'll come back as soon as she's adjusted," I told my department head and sometime lover, Cedric, when I first got here in February. "She's strong," I said.

"Do you want me to fly out over reading break?" he asked.

I edged the phone around the corner, out of Baba's hearing, and spoke as low as I could. "And do what?"

He hesitated, then said uncomfortably, "Well, I thought I could maybe help out with things. Just be around."

I had a brief and painful vision of him ruffling the afghan and scattering the pillows, while he and I watched Baba consume herself. "I can manage, thanks."

But I don't know if I can, and it's my own damn fault. I *had* help. A nurse supplied by the county who was looking after Baba when I arrived. Until I fired her for incompetence,

only to be told by the head of the agency how scarce a re-
source she was, how long the waiting lists for even an incom-
petent aide.

It's time to go. I place Baba's hands in her lap, settle the shawl
round her shoulders and hook it over the back of the wheelchair so it doesn't slip while I'm gone. Scan the room for anything that could hurt her while I'm not here to keep an eye on
her, to monitor those wandering hands.

"Ask him when he's coming home," she says, and I nod.

In the car I roll down the window, even though the radio says
the temperature is 24 below, a record low for March. The smells
in the house are getting to me. Once years ago, at the ballet, I
was seated beside a beautifully groomed woman of at least
ninety, powdered and scented and impeccably made up, and
I was thinking how nice it was of her granddaughter, maybe
great-granddaughter, to take her out, maybe away from an
old folks' home, for an evening. We smiled at each other as
the house lights dimmed, and then from beneath the pow-
dery scent of her perfume came a sudden sour smell. Decay. I
smell it on Baba now, in spite of perfume and powder and
baths.

Washing wasn't something I considered when I fired the
nurse: how difficult it would be for Baba to have me bathe
her, for me to see her naked, withered body. How nearly im-
possible to get near her meagre breasts and skiff of grey pubic
hair with the washcloth. How modesty clings to the psyche
even when so much else has vanished. After a couple of at-
tempts that ended with Baba raging and me rigid, and soapy
water everywhere, I've settled for sketchy sponge baths that
do little more than quiet my conscience.

Fortunately Baba can't smell herself. At least, if she can
she doesn't let on. Perhaps she catches the whiff of other things
from me, though. The two of us sniffing one another like

strange cats who have surprised each other on alien ground. I lean my face into the gust from the window, welcome the numbing of my ears, my nose.

Where Baba is in constant, furtive motion, secreting bits of herself within, burying them for who knows what future unearthing, Dido is still. All the activity that takes place goes on within; on the surface he is almost dead. Even the fluid that enters and leaves him shows no movement along the plastic tubes; a slight swelling at the needle's point of entry, that is all. The steady drip of the IV, the pulse of the monitor, are too far from that inert body to have any real connection with it. Baba's smell seems to come from her skin, from each pore, each cell. Dido's is easy to trace to the open mouth that puffs out, flaps in.

I sit beside him. I used to speak to him, hold his hand. They say people in his condition can feel and hear, just can't respond, but after the first month this gets hard to believe. Besides, I feel foolish talking to someone who can't even blink; it's like talking to myself. Or to a corpse. Of course, my silence is awkward too. Whenever a nurse walks by or smiles in at the still bed, I start smoothing the already smooth sheets, straightening the night table that holds only his false teeth and his watch. When one of them comes in to check the IV or update the chart, I clear my throat as though I am just finished speaking, or just about to speak.

I prefer the nurses who don't talk. The others, the ones who ask me questions or even chat to Dido, bounce off the silence in the room, in Dido, in me. Their speech becomes pointed, as though they are deliberately avoiding staring at a disability. Not Dido's. Mine.

"Let's tidy you up, Mr. Shemela. Make you look nice for your granddaughter, shall we?" Smoothing back the hair I should have smoothed. "It's really so good of you to keep coming, Miss Shemela. So many of our patients are left too much alone."

I nod, fingers at my lips tracing a knee-jerk smile. My lips are chapped. One of these days I'll simply go out for coffee or tea, read a book and toy with a pastry for an hour, and then go home and tell Baba what I always tell her anyway: no change.

The county nurse, Moira, she talked incessantly. On the rare occasions when she did pause, to sip tea or work on her nails, the house echoed with her. Even her clothing was loud. She didn't wear nurses' whites, came to the house every day in what she called her "mufti" — sweaters and slacks in various shades of purple, or in combinations of yellow and orange, her scratchy dyed-red hair scooped up into a matching nylon scarf. "Admin doesn't like us out of uniform, of course," she said with a wink, "but nurses are in short supply these days. Lots of us leaving for the States. And they loosen up a bit for us palliative care nurses — burnout rate's high enough, and that's the truth." And then she'd pull out a nail file and saw at her nails — one inch long, at least, and painted in all different colours, often two or three colours to a nail, and some of them with little fake jewels or bits of metal stuck on them. You had to wonder how much time she spent painting them. And how much time was left to care for Baba.

When she saw me staring at her nails, she fanned them out on the tabletop, where they looked almost severed from her fingers — as though someone had dropped a bag of those chocolate eggs wrapped in bright tinfoil. Moira examined them with critical pride. "Beautiful, aren't they? They're my sideline." She fished around in her sweater pocket and snapped a card onto the table. *Moira Jenson: Nail Sculpture and Repair. Manicures. Hand Massage.* "I took a beauty course in Edmonton a couple years back. Nursing's hard on the back and the feet, and when you're staring at the wrong side of fifty you start thinking about that." She reached for my hand and cradled it in her own, her nails meeting in a teepee over my square, blunt-trimmed fingers. "I could do you a real nice job. You'd need extensions, but that's a snap. Course, your cuticles are a mess — you've been picking at them, haven't you? —

but you just soak them in this special gel I've got and it softens them right up. You'd be surprised...."

I withdrew my hand and hid it in my pocket.

"Isn't it difficult to look after patients when you have such long nails? Say, bathing them, for example?" I should check Baba's body for scratches, I thought.

Moira grinned. "Never lost one yet. Not to these babies, anyway." She paused, then picked up the file. "Some of the old people like the feel of the nails on their skin. They may be out of it, but they still like to be touched. You know?"

Dido's skin is grey and flaccid. Each hair stands out against his skin too sharply. Unnaturally. I can almost trick myself into believing I see the hairs growing. The nurses do shave him but they can't possibly deal with his five o'clock shadow as quickly as he would himself. He always used a straight razor, pulled his skin taut with one hand, scraped slowly upward with the other. Smiled at me while I waited for the bathroom, his face bearded with white lather, his mouth twisted to one side, away from the tug of the blade. I wonder how the nurses manage to shave a face that offers no resistance, poke my finger into his cheek, watch it sink into the flesh, snatch it away when I hear the doctor closing the door behind him. Caught. Usually I manage to miss his rounds but today I left the house too late. A mental note for tomorrow.

"Good afternoon, Miss Shemela." He flips pages of Dido's chart. "Have you thought any more about what we discussed last week?"

The silence presses on us. I think I can hear Baba chewing, and shake my head. The doctor thinks I'm shaking at him.

"Have you talked it over with your grandmother? She is really the person to make the decision."

What kind of decision can you expect from someone who cannot remember two days together why her husband isn't home?

"Perhaps you could bring her in to see me," he says.

Dido should have something to listen to, I think, something to fill up these empty corners with sound.

"Or I could go talk to her at her home, if you like," says the doctor.

Beethoven. The Fifth booming through the house and Dido waving his arms in time, booming out the low notes himself in a deep, deep bass. I always preferred the Third, the Eroica.

"At the very least, you need to decide whether you want him resuscitated should he have a seizure. We need to have these things written on the chart."

This is the man who said I should talk to Dido in case he could hear. He looks at me expectantly.

"I was thinking of bringing in a radio tomorrow," I say. "If that's all right."

"Miss Shemela, I don't think you understand —"

When we brought Dido in here, Baba and I, it was early November. The busiest time of my term and, while I wanted to be here for both of them, I still chafed to be gone. Baba and I visited him every day, wheeled him around the hospital — to the cafeteria for rice pudding and coffee, to the big windows overlooking the reservoir, with the mountains in the distance. When the mandarin and satsuma oranges came in for Christmas, we took him some. They were his favourite. Baba sat beside him, peeling his orange for him, her fingers tearing through the porous, bubbled skin. Turning the peeled orange carefully in her hand, she picked away every shred of white pith, her fingers trembling slightly so that she sometimes had to take two or three tries at a white string before dropping it onto the neat pile on Dido's tray. Then she sectioned the orange, took one piece for herself, pressed another on me, placed one section in Dido's mouth. She held his hand as he chewed, the corners of his mouth moist with juice. I placed my hand on top of hers and felt its trembling, and told myself she was fine, just fine.

In the car I scroll the dial away from CBC, away from Jurgen Gothe's measured tones, to find the most raucous rock music possible. I don't recognize any of the songs, can't make out any of the words, and the yelling of the disc jockeys and the commercials curls my lip but is just what I need. There is not one corner of silence in this car. My ears hurt. My body edges towards movement, left hand patting the steering wheel, left foot tapping the brake pedal until the car behind honks its objections to my flaring, garbled Morse code. I surface to pain, a shred of chapped lip caught between my teeth.

The day I fired her, Moira suggested that I tie Baba's hands to the arms of the wheelchair — to give her fingers a rest, she said. I shook my head no and left to get some groceries. When I came back, Baba was in the kitchen, tied to her chair with two purple nylon scarves, while Moira painted her nails and listened to the radio. Baba and Dido have never had a television. "Television. Such nonsense," Baba would say, pulling a pan of holubtsi from the oven or shelling peas into a huge copper pan between her knees. "Waste of time." "Sshh," Dido would say, "listen to the music."

I stood in the doorway, unnoticed. Moira had changed the station from CBC to some country station. Hank Williams was whining his way through "I'm So Lonesome I Could Cry" and Moira was right in there with him, voice cracking on the high notes. Several jars of polish stood on the table in front of her, along with fluffs of cotton stained red and pink and orange. Moira painted one last careful sweep of the brush, stuffed the brush back in the bottle and screwed the top on with her palms. "There," she said to Baba. "What do you think? Maybe we could do something for you next time. You and your granddaughter. What you do to your hands is just criminal." She flicked her hands in front of her to dry the nails, then dangled her fingers in front of Baba.

Baba laughed. After days of chewing at herself and staring through me to the day when Dido would come home. "Such nonsense," she said to the dancing fingers, and laughed.

White heat shot through my body. I strode into the kitchen and snapped off the radio. Baba and Moira stared at me, Moira's hands frozen in front of her.

"I specifically asked you not to tie her up," I said, pressing myself hard into the countertop so she wouldn't see me shaking. "It's degrading. I want you out of here."

Moira lowered her hands to the table and gave me a measured look. "In the first place, you didn't say anything to me *specifically*. In fact, you hardly ever open your mouth. To me, or," she nodded in Baba's direction, "to her. In the second place...." She stopped and started to clatter her manicure implements and bottles into her bag. "Never mind."

"But I do mind." I was aching for a fight. "Tell me what you were going to say."

Moira hooked the bag over her shoulder, bent down to Baba and briefly stroked her fettered hand. "Goodbye, Mrs. Shemela. You take care, now."

Baba's face had returned to blankness, her lips working erratically over her teeth.

I followed Moira down the corridor, my heels thumping the hardwood. "Say what you mean, damn it."

"Very well, then. You've been in this house a week and I haven't seen you touch her once. Let alone kiss her or hold her. You act as though she has some kind of communicable disease instead of plain senility. And you talk to me about degrading."

"How dare you?"

As if she hadn't heard me, Moira propped one of her cards against the oak box on the mantel and said, "Keep this. You may not like the way I look or act, but at least I'm used to dealing with people like your grandmother. And whatever you think of me, your grandmother seems to like me."

"My grandmother doesn't know her own name from one day to the next. How could she possibly know what she likes?" The words were out before I could stop them. Appalled, I gave Moira one long naked look, then slammed the door on her.

That night I dreamt I was cleaning my apartment in Toronto. I opened the cupboard under the sink to find a room there I hadn't seen before that was filling with a sticky mess coming from the drain. I moved under the sink and found hundreds of afghans in bright purples and oranges, some of them made from what looked like human hair. The sticky mess licked at my toes so I started to stuff the afghans down the drain, one after the other, while it gurgled, "Tell me when you're coming home." And then Cedric appeared, and I held out my hand to him, thinking the drain wouldn't dare talk while he was here, the afghans were gone, we could be tidy now. And he took my hand in his but instead of pulling me out of the room he said, "Your fingers are a mess." And when I looked I saw the skin peeling off them in fragile ribbons, purple and orange.

I park the car in the narrow driveway, climb the few stairs and stand for a moment with my head pressed against the cold of the front door before turning my key in the lock. Baba sits as she did when I left. Her hands are in her lap, palms upward, fingers curling away from any snagging on the maroon wool shawl, which has slipped a few inches. A fleck of blood is on her cheek.

"When is he coming home?" she says. Her fingers rise to her mouth.

I pull Baba's hands into her lap and hold them there. They feel like tiny plucked birds. "Baba, we have to make some decisions," I say, and clear my throat. I can hear the sound of her quiet munching, but her hands are in mine. I shake my head to clear my ears.

"Baba, Dido is very sick." This is hopeless, we've been through this almost every day for the last three months. "The doctor wants us to make a decision. Actually, he wants me to make a decision. About Dido."

Baba's jawline trembles. She purses her lips tight. I grip her hands, feel the bones collide. I can hardly bear to touch her.

"I can't make the decision on my own, Baba. You have to help me. You have to speak to me about it."

Her fingers twitch in mine, her eyes flicker over the room

to the painted eggs on the cabinet. Black and red, flares of yellow. They look pretty from a distance but they are disappointing up close. Smudged, the lines that are supposed to separate the coloured sections blurred and broken. Baba and I made them together when I was twelve, and she has kept them all that time.

"Please, Baba. Please talk to me. Tell me what to do."

Baba's throat convulses. She opens her mouth, stares through me as her lower lip drops, and first there is a glint of something behind her teeth, then blood comes dribbling from her lip, white and red of blood and saliva over both our hands, pulpy grey shreds from the lining of her mouth sticking to my skin.

We stand in the kitchen, Baba and me. I am twelve. The egg feels grainy against my skin.

"Now, you hold it like this," says Baba, handing me a stylus and demonstrating with her own. It's like a fountain pen, with a metal tip and wooden handle. You can buy electric ones that keep the heat constant and the flow of wax steady, but Baba scorns them.

"Careful not to touch the tip," she says. "Hot." We hold our styluses, tips almost touching, in the flame of a red candle.

"Now dip in the wax." The ball of beeswax is a pale yellow lump on the table. The hot metal slides in without effort. Heating and dipping, we draw with wax on the rough egg surface, making crosses and triangles.

"The three sides are for thunder, sun and rain." Baba's wax lines are absolutely steady, her hand turning the egg with infinitesimal movement. "The crosses keep away sickness and evil."

My wax blots and blurs, my designs lose their shape, become crazy quadrangles. A blister rises on my finger where I touched the hot nib. Safeway is selling painted Easter eggs six for a dollar, and I tell Baba so.

"Not these eggs," says Baba. "These are pysanky." As

though that explains everything.

"There," she says. "Now for the dye."

There are dishes of dye on the table, yellow, orange, red and black.

"Yellow first," she says. "Always start with the lightest colours. Layer up to the darkest, see? Just like I put the dishes."

With a tablespoon we lower the eggs into the dye and leave them while we draw designs on two more. Lower those into yellow dye, remove the first two. Cover the yellow squares that are to stay yellow with more melted wax, leave the others exposed, dip into orange. Wax. Red. Wax. Finally black. The colours are drowning in layers of wax but we soak them in hot water, rub them with a soft cloth — "Gently now, gently. They break too easy," says Baba — and vivid colour emerges. A delicate layer of varnish on all but one, and they are finished.

"We make them for spring, to welcome the sun and new life," says Baba, her hand firm and damp under my chin, tilting it up to the smile in her eyes. "Without pysanky, darkness would flood the world." She releases my chin, puts each stylus in a narrow oak box. "Eggs from Safeway. Such nonsense!"

Then she calls Dido, and we sit at the kitchen table while Dido peels Baba's unvarnished pysanka, cuts it into three segments and gives one to each of us. Usually Baba makes a plain coloured egg for eating. Pysanky take too much time and effort, are too beautiful to waste. But this was the year of the crash that blew apart my life, the year I came, an orphan, to live with Baba and Dido, and Baba made this pysanka especially for me.

Baba's blood is drying on my skin. I smooth the hair from her unseeing eyes, raise her hands to my lips, inhale the smell of her age. The oak boxes are beside the painted eggs on the cabinet. I open one, weigh the stylus in my hand. Slight as it is, it seems to hold the weight of all my failures. My cracked lips sting with salt. (*Crying?* I can hear Baba in my head. *Crying? Such nonsense!*) A blur of white on the floor catches my eye.

I've knocked over Moira's card. *Moira Jenson: Nail Sculpture and Repair. Manicures. Hand Massage.* I run my tongue over the cracks in my lips, suck salt water. It feels as though the tears are not running into the cracks but seeping from them, and the taste of the tears is the bitter salt of longing. For Baba to soak my fingers in a thick warm gel, dry them with a soft towel and pare back the softened cuticle with a fine wooden stick. I want to feel her nails on my skin. I want her to cradle my blunt and clumsy fingers in her own, caressing them with infinitesimal care, ringing them round with perfect ovals painted all the colours of the rainbow, gleaming with gaudy points of light.

SURFACE SCRATCHES

On the morning of her fiftieth birthday, Claire woke to an insistent blaring in her ear. She flopped one arm over to Jack's side of the bed, then grabbed his empty pillow and her own and stuffed them on either side of her head. Useless. The horn blared on and on, until finally she staggered from the bed, snatched up her housecoat and stumbled into the morning to find out what all the ruckus was about.

There was Jack, in track suit and parka, standing beside a steel-grey bullet of a car, leaning in the driver's window to press the horn, while the next-door neighbours looked on from their porch, applauding, laughing.

"What is this? What are you doing?" She waved half-heartedly at the neighbours, trying to push her hair into some kind of order and draw her dressing gown more closely round her body to choke off the shrill January wind.

"Happy birthday, honey!" Jack planted a showy kiss on her mouth, and pressed a set of keys into her hand, folding her fingers around the scratchy metal. "It's all yours." He left a pause for some kind of reaction; then, when none was forthcoming, proclaimed, "It's a Jag!"

"Happy fiftieth, Claire!" the neighbours called, stamping their feet in the cold.

She turned to Jack, taking in his flushed face, the bravado of his stance, the slight rocking on his feet.

"Where's my station wagon?"

"I traded it in this morning while you were asleep." His face got redder. Things obviously weren't going as he had planned. Claire felt a stab of pity.

"It's wonderful, Jack. Thank you." She hugged him for the neighbours, who waved once more and hurried back into their house.

"That's more like it." Jack was smiling, but he had lost his earlier heartiness. "I knew you'd love it."

Claire softened. "Let me get dressed," she said giving his arm a squeeze. "Then you can take me for a test drive."

As they walked past the front of the car, the jaws of the jaguar hood ornament were open and laughing.

That afternoon a slim parcel arrived special delivery from their daughter. A Queen Elizabeth fridge-magnet set, with a complete wardrobe from suburban-look pillbox hat and skirt suit to tiara, mink wrap and dazzling evening gown. The birthday card featured a photograph of a wizened granny in sky-diving gear, and read, "Today is the first day of the rest of your life." Claire winced. At the bottom of the card was a hasty scrawl — *Happy Birthday Mom!* Rachelle had signed for the twins as well, no doubt knowing they'd forget.

Claire freed the Queen from her cellophane wrap, then placed her in the centre of the bare white fridge, sticking the clothes around her at random. It looked as though there had been an explosion at a fancy-dress ball. She frowned, then stacked the clothes layer upon layer over Queen Elizabeth, the evening gown spilling out from beneath the knee-length suit.

Claire sat at the kitchen table. Jack was outside polishing the Jag with a chamois. He had already warned her not to take it through a carwash, not even to wash it herself since she might not lather up enough, and hidden dust motes could ruin the sheen.

She sighed and flipped through the Continuing Education calendar that had arrived that morning. Perhaps a course would shake her out of the doldrums she'd been in the last while. Maybe tai chi. Except she felt her life was already moving in slow motion. Her fingers hovered over the creative-writing page. Once, years ago, she had started a novel. A romance. They'd needed money and she'd thought, if she could knock one off, she could take some of the pressure off Jack. And it was something she could do at home, in between caring for the baby and doing the books for the business. But then the twins had come, and she'd put the novel aside and never picked it up again. She hadn't thought of it in years.

Two weeks later, when she went into Jack's study to tell him she was off to her first class, Jack was poring over brochures for Belize. His partner, Garth, was taking a new girlfriend there and wanted to make the trip a foursome.

"But Jack," Claire protested, "I haven't even met her!"

"You know you get along with everybody," he said absently. "You'll love her. Besides, you like Garth." Claire decided to let that one pass. "I'll tell you what. We'll have them for dinner before we go. Give you two a chance to get to know one another."

What's the point? Claire thought. I barely get to know their names before he moves on to the next one. "I have to go to class. Let's talk it over later, OK?"

"Sure thing." He was flipping between pamphlets, but as she left the room he looked up long enough to call, "Don't forget to park across two spaces!"

Claire threw her bookbag onto the passenger seat, then turned on the ignition. Even after two weeks, she wasn't comfortable with the car. It wasn't that she resented Jack's trading in her station wagon, which had been showing its age for some time. But when she'd thought of a new car, her mind had wandered towards something like the Miatas, with their jelly-bean colours and contours, or the new Volkswagens. The first car they had ever owned had been a Beetle. She still smiled to think how funny he'd looked folding his long frame into that round, red car.

She eased out cautiously into the street. There was a skiff

of snow on the road, but that wasn't what worried her. She was a competent driver. But although her habits hadn't changed since getting the Jag, she could swear that other drivers were treating her differently. She had been cut off more times than she could count in the last two weeks, and honked at, too, as though the drivers had an image of someone in the Jag who didn't resemble Claire at all. "I'm a nice person!" she wanted to shout. "It wasn't even my choice! It's my husband's mid-life crisis, not mine!" Except that Jack didn't appear to be having a crisis. He appeared to be having the time of his life.

At a red light on Crowchild Trail, she glanced at the Bronco on her right and wondered what had ever happened to the energy crisis. The crisis that had almost destroyed Jack's fledgling seismic business, and had kept Claire pondering over the books late into the night after Jack had to fire the bookkeeper. They had driven their VW practically into the ground, until rust had eaten a hole in the floor on the driver's side and you had to remember to lay plastic down before you drove in the rain. Small cars had been all the rage back then; conservation the new watchword. Now recycling was the watchword, and everyone drove to the recycling bins in gas guzzlers.

Claire surfaced from her musings to a persistent revving in her left ear. A young man with jet-black hair and a silver earring was gunning his Firebird, jutting his chin at her, until she rolled down the tinted windows to show him that she wasn't the kind of person to be interested in a race. He squealed through the intersection as soon as the light changed, and Claire held well back until he vanished.

In the classroom, half a dozen people doodled on scratch pads or wrote furiously in dog-eared notebooks. They were all much younger than Claire. A fawnlike young woman, who seemed to be a soft golden-beige from hair to toe, kept her head ducked towards her desk. Another, with purple and green twists of hair sprouting all over her head, smiled at Claire and then quickly looked away. A young man all in black, with a dangly silver earring, drummed on his desk with a pencil. For a moment she thought he was the man in the Firebird, but he didn't look at her so it was hard to be sure. For all she knew, this was the current uniform of the young; since her boys had left home she'd fallen out of touch.

She took a seat towards the back of the room. Almost immediately the door slammed shut and a man strode to the front, dressed in a frayed fisherman's jersey and baggy corduroys. He ran a hand through dark hair threaded with grey, shot his dark eyes over the lot of them and said, throwing his books on the desk, "So. You want to write."

Minutes later, they were writing. "Write!" he thundered at them. "Twenty minutes' timed writing, starting now."

All the others ripped to a fresh sheet of paper and started tearing across it with pens and pencils, heads bent in concentration. The instructor strode back and forth in front of the blackboard, tossing out remarks like "Nothing is boring! Everything is vital! Everything is grist for the mill of art."

Art, Claire thought, staring at the blank page in front of her. Was that what she was doing?

She made a stab at the white space with the fountain pen Jack had given her all those years ago, when she'd said she wanted to write. Even though she'd put a fresh cartridge in this morning, the pen was dry, and she had to shake vigorously to get the ink flowing. The first marks on her page were the blobs of ink that finally flew from the nib.

"Dig deep!" boomed the instructor. "All of us know passion, tragedy, comedy. Let yourself go!"

Claire had written two pages by the time he said, "Time's up."

"My name is Frank Jameson," he announced. "I'm not here to tell you that you have genius or potential or even anything interesting to say. I'm here to make you work your damnedest." He leaned on the desk and pointed to the fawn-coloured girl. "You. Give us your name and then read some of what you've written."

"I'm Susan," she said almost inaudibly. "I didn't know we'd have to read, I don't know ... it's so personal ..." Jameson unbent slightly. "Fine — you can show it to me on break just this once."

Claire didn't hear much of what each person read. Her stomach was gurgling, her ears filling with noise. She surfaced briefly when the spiky-haired girl, Jonesy, read about waking in the night to an eerie presence by the bed. Then it was Claire's turn.

"Well," she said, after giving her name, "I always wanted to write a romance, but then the children came and ..."

"Just read, Claire," Jameson waved a lazy hand. "Let your work do your talking for you."

Claire dove into the opening to her novel. She'd started out promisingly enough, she thought: "People assumed that Magenta was named for her glorious red hair, but really she was named for the sunrise her father saw on the morning he hit his first gusher." In the first paragraph, Claire neatly killed off both Magenta's parents and introduced an oil-baron hero. But then she got sidetracked by the hero's car, a Jaguar, and wrote at some length about how older cars used to have round, innocent headlight eyes and grinning grille plates, as though Disney had had a hand in the design. Now they looked like predators, and were named for them, too. She was the last to read, so it could have been mere coincidence that Jameson said, "Now we move to the next phase. Yes, you must write what you know, but at some point you must step back and ask yourself the truly important question: So what?"

When Claire got to her car, there was a ragged note under the windshield wiper: *You Prick*.

The lot was crammed with cars. She crumpled the note in her hand and stuffed it into her pocket.

When she got home, Jack waved the travel pamphlets triumphantly. "We're booked! First class all the way!"

Claire handed him the note.

"What the hell...?" Jack scrambled up off the couch.

"Someone left this on my windshield. I told you people don't like it if you park across two spaces. I never did."

Jack crushed the note with his fist and tossed it on the coffee table. "Just ignore it. If that car gets dinged it's an easy five thou to repair it. You can't just touch it up, you know."

Claire opened her mouth to protest further, but he threw an arm around her and gave her a squeeze. "This is going to be a blast! Nothing but the best — hotels, limos, the works! You're gonna love it! Oh," he added, "I remembered what you said about wanting to get to know Ashley — so I invited them for dinner a week Friday."

Oh well, thought Claire, How bad could it be? Besides, she could look on the trip as research for her novel. The perfect exotic backdrop for her heroine.

For most of that week, Claire wrote every day, as Jameson had instructed. The first day, Jack suggested she turn one of the bedrooms into a study, but she preferred to write at the kitchen table while he was at work. The second day, he brought a laptop from the office. "If you want, you can move around the house. You can even take it out to the gazebo and write there!"

"Actually, I think I like writing by hand," she said, holding up the fountain pen. "But thank you."

The third day he asked if he could read what she'd written so far and, after doing so, suggested she make the hero a seismic company owner instead of an oil baron. He seemed a bit hurt when Claire explained that a gusher was more exciting than a small underground explosion, that striking oil had far more dramatic impact than simply scanning seismographic records for the possibility of its presence. "But I could think about it," said Claire reluctantly, kicking herself for this need to speak when she didn't want to, to rush into silence with mouth flapping and brain two steps behind, smoothing over any signs of dissension or hurt feelings.

"Sure thing," he said, but his face was closed, and he didn't offer any more suggestions after that.

Claire got to her second class a bit early, to find the door shut.

Through the window she could see Jameson with Susan, their heads bent close together over her work, so Claire sat down to wait on a bench in the hall, bookbag balanced in her lap. A young woman with black hair, dressed all in black, strode up to the door of the classroom, stopped, heaved a great sigh and plunked down by Claire on the bench.

"Hi," she said glumly.

Claire looked hard at the young woman and realized with a start that it was Jonesy, but a Jonesy who bore no resemblance to her former self. She had traded in her green and purple spikes for a jet-black mop, and had powdered her face a flat, vampirish white. Her lips were black, her eyes heavily lined, and black-varnished nails clicked against the can of Coke she pulled out of her cavernous knapsack.

"I'm sorry," said Claire, "I didn't recognize you."

"That's great!" Jonesy's smile creased her white paint. "I come to class straight from one of my jobs — at Second Time Around. I like to try out different looks." She waved a hand over herself with a magician's flair. "Most times I just borrow the clothes and put them back before the manager notices."

"Couldn't that get you into trouble?"

"Oh, yeah," Jonesy said airily, "but what's life without a little trouble?" She looked hopefully around the bare hallway, then slumped against the wall and scuffed her army-booted feet on the floor.

"You said you had another job...?" Claire prodded gently.

"Yeah — two others, actually. All part-time. One's at ..." The classroom door opened. Jonesy stiffened and her gaze fixed over Claire's right shoulder. Jameson and Susan came out of the classroom and wandered down the hall without a glance in their direction.

"He's pretty neat, isn't he?" Jonesy's wistful tone was so at odds with her teeth gleaming white through black lips that Claire had to hold back a laugh. "I suppose so."

"He knows so *much*. About writing, but more than that...." Jonesy clutched her inky hair with ebony-tipped fingers. "He just makes me want to write something that knocks him sideways." She looked up from between fists of tortured hair that Claire had an urge to stroke with a taming hand. But Jonesy shook herself and laughed, threw her bag over her shoulder and headed for the classroom.

"Right," Jameson said when he came back into the room. "Let's hear it." And he pointed at Claire to begin.

Claire had followed Jameson's instructions to the letter: "Write a full page in which you evoke an emotion without naming it." She had found it difficult to pick an emotion, but by the end of the week, when she had written nothing, she decided hunger would have to do, and sent Magenta down the long corridors of the mansion to ask the cook for a snack. But she couldn't seem to get her fiery-tressed heroine back out of the kitchen, and ended up writing a long digression about the cook, a stocky, grey-haired woman who was clarifying butter: "the crusted foam rising to the top, the butter snapping and snarling as it bubbled from the base of the pot." Claire salivated while she read but, when she finished, one of the students muttered something about "kitchen sink nihilism." This made no sense to Claire but it couldn't be good, because Jonesy, who seemed a gentle soul behind all the violent makeup, frowned at him. Jameson merely motioned to Jonesy to read.

Jonesy's passage depicted a young girl's ambulance ride to Emergency, her drugged-out mother leaking tubes and vomit and a stream of verbal poison. "The girl thinks herself away," Jonesy read, eyes closed, "out and away, into the paramedics beside her, the nurses who wheel her mother down the long corridor, the actresses on the TV shows she watches while she waits for news. She dreams herself into safety, into the arms of a mother she's never known."

In the parking lot Claire heard a call from behind, "Hey Claire! Wait up!" Jonesy was flying towards her, a tangle of bouncing black hair and banging backpack and chunky boots. She fell into step beside Claire, breathing in gusts.

"Anger, right?" Powder drifted from her face, creating shiny motes in the streaks of parking lot light.

"What?"

"Your piece, the butter, I mean. Sounded like anger — all that snarling and snapping."

"Oh. I don't know. I hadn't really thought about it that way."

"Oh well, never mind. It just struck me, that's all. Did you guess mine?"

"I thought — loneliness?"

Jonesy laughed. "No — fear! That's what I was aiming at!" She swiped at a nose dripping with cold, her hand taking a bit of white paint with it, revealing a red glow beneath. "Well, I guess we both have a long way to go, don't we?"

Claire laughed too. "I guess so."

"Pretty neat assignment for next week — the last chapter of our biography. I sort of see myself in a garret somewhere, like, a lonely alcoholic." Her voice sounded remarkably cheery given such a grim look into the future, and Claire once again felt the urge to laugh, but decided she didn't know Jonesy well enough. Then, with a sudden rush of feeling, she decided that she would like to, and she opened her mouth to ask if Jonesy wanted to grab a coffee, Claire's treat.

But Jonesy cut her off, distracted by the sight of the Jag parked across two spaces.

"God," she said with a grimace of her vampirish face, "some people are such bastards, aren't they?" She turned a blinding smile on Claire. "Where are you parked? That's me in the corner." She pointed to an ancient VW bug convertible that had once been white with a black and white checkered hood, but was now more than half rust. Claire didn't even glance at the Jag as she said, in a parody of a dithery old lady, "My goodness, I just realized I parked on another level!" She walked back towards the exit, waving cheerily to Jonesy, and hid behind a pillar until the bug roared and sputtered off the lot.

Claire thought about the last chapter of her life while she peeled and sliced mushrooms, crushed Tillicherry peppercorns with the cleaver and rubbed them into deep red tenderloin. She boiled down the tarragon vinegar and shallots, beat in first the egg yolks, then knob after knob of butter. Claire enjoyed cooking for others, their murmurs of pleasure, of praise. Whatever her feelings about Garth, the man knew good food when he tasted it. Her eyes lost their focus on the practised ease of her hands; she saw herself rising from her deathbed to sprinkle minced Italian parsley on baby potatoes boiled in their jackets. Blinking away the vision, she ran it and the mushroom peelings down the sink with a vicious blast from the sprayer, then wiped her hands on her apron and went upstairs to change.

"Aren't you ready yet?" Jack was fussing with his hair, combing it back and forth over the thinning patch on top.

"It won't take me long." She slipped into the dress she'd left waiting on the bed, plain but exquisitely cut. Smoothed it appreciatively over her hips.

"That's nice," Jack said. "What jewellery are you going to wear?"

Claire rummaged through her jewellery box. In the early years of their marriage she hadn't noticed that she and Jack had differing taste in jewellery, because he could never afford to buy her any. Later on, when his business improved, she was surprised to find that his taste in presents leaned towards the showy — heavy gold chains, large rings crusted with diamond chips, chunky bracelets that made a woman as short and stocky as Claire look weighed down, eclipsed. But he always looked so pleased with his latest find that she didn't like to say she preferred the understated. So every year, at Christmas and her birthday, she thanked him and locked the gifts away in her jewellery box.

The crowning absurdity was the mink coat he had given her last Valentine's. It wasn't only that she felt uncomfortable in the skin of a dead animal — in the seventies she had taken Rachelle in her stroller on a protest march against the fur trade. Apart from that, she looked like a bloated hedgehog in the thing. Which made her wonder what woman Jack was really buying all these things for. Who he saw when he looked at her.

"They're just pulling into the drive." Jack was looking out the bedroom window. "Are you ready?"

Claire put on a diamond dinner ring and the pearl necklace her mother had left her, then followed him downstairs. She opened the door to Garth and Ashley and came face to face with Magenta. The fine-spun coppery hair, the creamy skin, the violet eyes, the mink that caressed a delicately sculpted chin. "Hello," said Claire and, feeling as if she were walking into her own novel, she reached out to shake Ashley's hand.

The dinner was not a success. Ashley picked at her hot scallop salad as though looking for bugs, nibbled a shred of lettuce, then laid down her fork as though exhausted, saying to Garth with a smile, "You know what a small appetite I have. I can't finish my dinner if I eat too much of the first course." But she barely touched her main course either. Just patted her tummy and said, "That's lots, thanks. Got to think about squeezing into the old bikini in Belize!" Claire flinched. She had never worn a bikini. When they first became fashionable she was pregnant, and later she was sensitive about her stretch marks.

Garth ate only a few mouthfuls of steak, spurned the mushrooms and potatoes and asked for bare lettuce with low-fat dressing on the side instead of the Caesar salad. He settled for yogurt when Claire explained that she didn't keep bottled dressings in the house. In the end he left most of it on his plate. Even Jack left a few potatoes uneaten.

When Jack and Garth took their coffee and brandy to the living room, Ashley looked at them uncertainly, then trailed after Claire into the kitchen and perched uncomfortably on a stool at the counter while Claire cleaned up.

"I'm glad we planned this trip for later in March," she said, while Claire shovelled steak Béarnaise and sautéed mushrooms and parsleyed potatoes into the garburator. "I'm having this laser surgery done and I can't go anywhere for a few days afterwards."

"Surgery? Are you sure you'll be all right in time to go?" Hope flared briefly in Claire's heart.

"Oh, not major surgery. It's like a minor facelift. They burn away the top two or three layers of your skin with laser light."

"Doesn't it hurt?"

"They freeze you before they do it, and they give you Tylenol 3s. It's like a really bad sunburn. That's what they say, anyway." Ashley toyed with her delicate emerald necklace, a present from Garth.

"A really bad sunburn that you have to take prescription painkillers for? What does it do?"

"Takes away all the little wrinkles. You know — laugh lines, worry lines." Claire looked at Ashley's smooth and glowing skin, the barest of crow's feet at the corners of her eyes. "I was thinking I'd like to have the liposuction done too, but there's no time before we go." Ashley handed a plate to Claire. "Pity."

Ashley must have seen some of Claire's incredulity on her face, because she laughed and said, "Oh, I know I'm not fat! It's just that when I gain a pound it goes right here." She patted her thighs. "I work out like crazy, too."

Claire put the plate in the dishwasher, leaning far over to hide her face. She felt a wild laugh building in her, one that had nothing to do with amusement.

"Garth is an investor in the clinic so I'm getting it done for free. Actually, that's how I met Garth. He hired me to set up the accounting procedures."

"Oh, I didn't know."

"Yeah. Garth is thinking of getting a laser job himself. But he's got to plan it more carefully. He'd have a deeper burn — ten layers. You can't go anywhere for two weeks while you heal. It could infect really easily, and besides, you wouldn't want anyone to see you — I guess the scabs kind of weep for the first little while. Well, it's a third-degree burn, after all. But they say it takes off five years."

Claire felt sick to her stomach. "You know," she said with a thin smile, "I'm about done in here. Why don't you go join the others. I'll be there in a minute." And she flipped on the garburator before Ashley could reply.

Over coffee and liqueurs Claire watched Garth sip his brandy and tried to picture his square, chiselled face covered with weeping sores. She followed his blunt fingers moving from bottle to glass and thought, I have never liked him, I have merely tolerated him. For thirty years. Claire helped herself liberally to brandy. You're one in a long line of trade-ins, honey, her mind pulsed towards Ashley, who was leaning in close to Garth, laughing at all his jokes. He'll be back, Claire mumbled into her brandy snifter. You'll be gone and he'll be back, probably healing from third-degree burns, back like he is after every breakup, looking for roast beef and baked potatoes with sour cream, home cooking and sympathy. Thanking me for apple pie without ever really looking at me.

Later that night, Claire lay beside Jack and counted his breaths, usually a surefire way to get to sleep. But tonight her eyes burned wide open, her body pulsed with heat. How could he sleep? He was the seismic expert. How was it he couldn't detect the detonations going off in the body right next to him? For what seemed the first time in years, Claire took stock of that body. She ran her hands over the greying hair she had kept cropped short since she first had the kids. She probed the wrinkles round her eyes, the loose skin at her jowls, the lines of her scars — appendectomy, C-section. Explored the breasts that never went back to their original shape after breastfeeding, the belly that poked out the pleats of her pants. Until tonight, she thought of her body as making space, developing "give," a comfortable, loose fit. Letting go. "Let yourself go," Jameson had said that first night, but Claire doubted he meant what Ashley surely thought when she looked at Claire with those clear, unwrinkled eyes.

When she finally slept, Claire dreamed that she was in an enormous leather-bound book, and that Jack was pounding on the cover, screaming, "Let me in! Let me in!" Magenta was about to push open the book, but Jonesy tackled her and pinned her to the page. Claire squeezed in close to the spine with the cook, the two of them squashed almost flat by the pages, while the cook wrote out a recipe in a cramped hand and a language that Claire couldn't read.

Throughout the next few weeks in Jameson's class, Claire struggled to breathe life into her novel. Susan fled the class in tears at mid-term. Jonesy flitted through a persona a week: a flaming redhead in leopard-skin tights and black spike heels, a platinum blonde in tight bodice and flared skirt. Claire hoped for another conversation with her, but at the end of every class Jonesy bolted to the front to show her latest work to Jameson.

Claire's work he commented on briefly, save for one night when he pulled her aside and said, "I know you want to write a romance novel, so I should tell you to cut all these digressions about the cook and her chauffeur husband. But they're the only parts that are even semi-interesting. Do you see?" He pointed to a passage where the chauffeur had just thrown out several months' worth of newspapers that his wife had saved because she was too busy looking after Magenta and the mansion to find time to read. "There's tremendous comedic potential here." Claire stared blankly at the page, then at Jameson, whose face shut down. "Just keep going," he said dismissively. "Keep delving."

The fact was, Claire was losing interest in her novel. She sat for long hours at the kitchen table, staring into space, doodling or rearranging the clothes on Queen Elizabeth. One afternoon she looked up to find Jack standing in the doorway watching her.

"Why don't we go buy some clothes for the trip?" he said. "We leave next week, you know."

Claire had drawn detachable breasts and pubic hair for the Queen, and was starting on a detachable heart and lungs and stomach. But something about Jack made her stop in mid-stroke.

"Is your hair getting darker?"

He blushed.

"My God, it is. You're using something, aren't you? Grecian Formula." A few years back, Garth's hair had edged towards grey, then sidled back to a dark blond. She and Jack had laughed about it at the time. Jack ran a hand nervously over his thinning spot.

It had been a long time since they had laughed like that, Claire realized. Together. At the same time. A wave of heat started in her mid-chest and exploded in her brain.

"That's it. I'm not going to Belize."

"What? Because I'm using Grecian Formula? I only just ..."

"I know. You only just did it because Garth tried it. Did you know he's going to burn away half his face? Did he tell you that?"

"No. I mean, I knew he invested in this new laser business, but he's always got lots of irons in the fire, you know that. What does this have to do with Belize?"

"I don't want to go with them. I don't want to go anywhere with them."

"Well, that's great. At this late date. You could have told me sooner."

"I tried to tell you, but you went ahead and booked it anyway. And you knew I had signed up for this class." Even Claire knew this was a foolish jab. She hated the class. She'd been thinking of dropping it for weeks.

"Look, Claire, I've been looking forward to this trip for months. You know how hard things have been at work lately. I need this break."

"If that isn't just like you. You need the break, so I'm supposed to put aside whatever I'm doing."

He picked up her doodles. "Yes, I can see what you're doing. Think you'll sell the movie rights?"

"Give that to me!" Claire snatched the pad of paper out of his hand. "It's just like the newspapers!"

"What?"

"Back when the twins were born. I never got the time to

read the papers. I set them aside so they'd be there when I could get to them and *you threw them out!*"

"When the twins were babies? What are you talking about?"

"I set everything aside. And now you're trying to make yourself look years younger. For who? How will I look, married to a man without wrinkles? Or do you want me to go and burn off half my face too? Maybe you're planning to trade me in, the way Garth does?"

"Claire, you're getting carried away. All I did was use some hair stuff."

But Claire was on a roll. "And another thing. I don't like that car! I have never liked that car. I want a Miata." She sounded like a spoiled child, even to herself. But she had hit a sore spot. Jack's face turned hard and red as a brick.

"Well, why didn't you say so?"

"Because I didn't want to hurt your feelings. I never want to hurt your feelings."

"Guess you're making up for it now, aren't you?" He took a moment to pull himself together. "Look. It doesn't matter about the car. I'll just lease one you like."

"Oh, my God." Claire got up and began to pace around the room. "You leased it. My birthday present. How could you?"

"Look, Claire, it's no big deal. Garth said it was a way to drive a terrific car without a huge up-front investment. And when you do it through the company, it's tax-deductible."

"You gave me a tax-deductible present?"

"You know, Claire," Jack said evenly, as if he too was aware of a line being crossed, "you never seem to like any of the presents I give you. So I thought I might as well get *something* out of it."

He left the room as though he were making an entrance rather than an exit, entering a world into which Claire didn't want to follow. But what would happen to her, and to Jack, if she stayed behind?

In the end, Jack went to Belize with Garth and Ashley, and God knew who else, and Claire wound up driving alone in an unfamiliar part of town for the final class reading which Jameson had arranged to hold in a blues bar he frequented. The parking lot was crowded with motorcycles and vans, a couple of the oldest ones painted with big-breasted cave-women crouching over fresh kill, or big-breasted angels rising from darkened plains. Claire didn't dare park across two spaces here, and she felt a certain defiant pleasure in putting the precious lease car at risk. As she walked towards the door of the pub she felt the neat press of her trousers, the matching blue pumps and jacket, marking her like a brand.

Through the greasy front window she saw the blurred outline of a young woman seated on a stool, a sheaf of papers on her lap, holding a microphone close to her mouth. But she was facing the window, her back to the audience. Claire walked into the pub as quietly as she could and found a seat at the back. The young woman's vaguely familiar voice read lines about breasts and nipples and making love in the afternoon and world peace and giving birth to a new age. The words drifted past Claire's ears without taking hold. For a moment she thought Susan had rejoined the class at the last minute. Then the woman stopped reading, turned and ducked away from the brief applause. Claire gaped.

It was Jonesy. Wearing a long, clinging dress in forest green, her hair a soft brown cloud, her face touched up with, at most, sheer foundation and blush. The only thing Claire recognized was the army boots. Jonesy left the stage to be extravagantly hugged by the others, then went up to Jameson, who was dressed in dark jacket and pants, a fringed white silk scarf tossed round his neck. She smiled shyly, leaned in to whisper something, and he squashed her against him, bending her at the waist to mould her to his side, his fingers splayed to cover her from waist to just beneath her breast. She gazed up at him in a blaze of devotion. He released her and mounted the stage, reading a poem about, of all things, spit. Thanked them for coming. Said good night.

Claire folded her piece of paper up small and stuffed it to the bottom of her bag. Her cheeks were burning. She had thought her outfit would make her conspicuous and had instead discovered she was invisible. It was not just that no one even wondered where she might be. It was that when she looked at them a certain light pulsed around them, a light of youth and arrogance and conviction that all things began with them, that all discoveries before them had been purely preliminary. Claire's poem, the first she had ever written, about a flash of connection with an ashen-faced, black-lipped young woman, seemed ridiculous to her now.

She left the bar without anyone seeing her. The Jag gleamed in the faint light from the bar windows. Keys in hand, she had an impulse to scrape its smug and flawless surface, but instead she unlocked the door and got inside. When she turned the ignition, twelve cylinders hummed to life, throbbing through her hands on the wheel, her feet on the pedals, even snaking through the seat into her groin. It was funny, she had to admit. All this power and nowhere to go. But the laugh was dangerously close to tears, and she knew that wherever she decided to go, she didn't want to be here. She threw the car into reverse, trod on the gas and, forgetting to check her rearview mirror, banged into the car behind her. Jonesy's VW. Damn. Not that Jonesy would notice another dent on that battered vehicle. Putting the car into drive, Claire eased forward, felt the tug on her rear bumper as the cars disengaged, felt adrenalin bubble up from deep in her chest.

She got out of her car to check the damage to the Jag. A nice round dent, the paint creased, bare metal glinting from beneath the grey surface. Claire smiled. It felt more like hers already. She scrounged in her handbag for paper and pen. "Jonesy," she wrote, "I'm fessing up. I am the prick with the Jag who just banged into your car. But more importantly, Jonesy — whatever you do, whoever you love, hang onto your army boots."

She slipped the note under a windshield wiper. One week before Jack came back from Belize. One week to think of how to explain to him that a few dings and dents and scratches were not only inevitable but desirable things in a car. In a life. But the first thing to do was to get into her car, open her up, and put a few miles on her. See what she could do. Claire smiled, and aimed the leaping ornament at the open road.

The Gift of Tongues

Judy sprays a cloud of cologne in front of her, then dances through it, growling the tune to "Wild Thing" through pursed lips. She zips up her black leather skirt, does a bit of a bump and grind, slinks into matching leather vest, and checks her watch. Not enough time to phone Tabitha before she leaves. She'll have to wait till lunchtime tomorrow to tell her and the other wild things all about her date.

It was the guys on the football team who first started calling them "the wild things," growling the song after them in the halls while Judy and her friends flicked their hair and laughed. They take over the can at lunchtime, the wild things, sitting on the floor, eating their sandwiches and smoking cigarettes, coolly eyeing the other girls who come in to use the toilets. She can just hear their howls when she tells them that Paul Leudy the A student, Paul the guy who barely says boo from one day to the next, has asked her out on a date.

Judy leans into the mirror, fluffs her blonde hair, then heavy-lids her eyes with jet-black liner and mascara and rouges her lips deep red. If he's looking for a temptress, she'll give him his money's worth. She puckers up to a wad of Kleenex. Might even be fun.

Judy clatters down the stairs and her mother calls from the living room, "Where are you going?"

"Out," Judy says. This is all Judy ever tells her mother. Out. Deal with it.

And as per usual her mother appears in the doorway and says, "Not dressed like that, you're not." Then turns back to her tumbler of what looks like orange juice but is really a screwdriver. Judy's mother starts her liquid diet at ten in the morning so by this time of day, even though she talks big, she's pretty harmless. Judy usually takes off before her dad comes home. Saves her listening to him reading her mother the riot act about AA, or saying he's had a bitch of a day and joining her in drowning sorrows. Their business, but why should Judy have to stick around to watch? Her two older brothers cut out as soon as they could get steady work, and so will she. Just one more year of school and then she'll be gone gone gone and, like her brothers, she won't be back.

The doorbell rings and she snatches up jacket and purse and yells over her shoulder, "Don't wait up!"

Paul doesn't talk much on their walk to the theatre. He's different from any other guy she's dated, no smartass remarks, and he hasn't touched her once, not even when he helped her with her jacket. She'll laugh about this when she tells Tabitha tomorrow, but really she finds it kind of sweet. He has blond hair and eyes so deep a blue that Judy thinks she could dive right into them and swim around with his thoughts. She wonders if he remembers that she had a terrible crush on him in elementary school. Eight or nine years old, she screwed up her courage and offered him a packet of candies, small hard pink and blue nuggets, in the cloakroom after class. Paul looked around at his snickering friends and then waved the package in a wide arc, candies spraying the cloakroom, bouncing off the walls and floor into galoshes and under wooden benches. Judy felt her heart crack with them. *Ping ping ping.* Tabitha picked up as many of the pieces as she could, and shielded Judy from the teacher's inquisitive eye while Judy cried into her gym socks. What a sap, she thinks now, embarrassing Paul in front of his friends like that. She hopes he's forgotten it.

To Judy's surprise, instead of going to a movie theatre

they end up at a community centre, rows of iron chairs in front of a portable screen, a reel-to-reel perched on a rickety metal stand and a man in a dark suit and white collar greeting everyone at the entrance. Paul's father. He stiffens when Paul introduces him to Judy, one flick of his eyes taking in her outfit, her makeup. She feels her spine and face muscles calcify in response, her adrenalin start a slow burn. This is the kind of challenge the wild things relish, but who'd have figured Paul had it in him, bringing a wild thing in to bug his father. Judy puts an extra swing in her hips as they take their seats.

The movie is about some guy who falls for a Christian girl who won't date him unless he is "saved." Judy settles in for a boring time of it, figuring Paul was a bit of a jerk not to tell her what kind of movie he was taking her to, but what the hell, it's two hours out of her life, max. There's a moment of interest when the girl reads a poem called "The Hound of Heaven" and Judy gets a kick out of picturing God as the Hound of the Baskervilles, snarling and slavering and menacing, while she sits in the dark breathing in Paul's scent. But then the girl starts talking about the love of Christ which embraces all people, no matter who they are or what they've done, and in spite of herself Judy starts paying attention. Love isn't a word she considers very often. Especially this kind of love. Her brothers she rarely sees, her parents she avoids. What she feels for the wild things is not so much love as self-defence. Except for Tabitha who's been her best friend since elementary school. Tabitha who knew firsthand what it meant to walk through the door after school, wondering whether it would be a good day or a bad day. A good day meant supper on the stove, mother upright and perhaps smiling; a bad day was an empty vodka bottle on the table, and potatoes to peel so Dad wouldn't burst a gasket when he got home. You had to toughen up to live in this world, was nine-year-old Tabitha's advice, and Judy had clung to it, and to Tabitha, for seven years. So when Paul takes her hand gently in his, she is shocked to find herself hollow with longing and, as if that isn't bad enough, she's crying, first ragged intakes of breath, then, as he strokes her palm with his thumb, sobs that empty her even more, and in the outrush are her parents, her brothers, even Tabitha and the wild things, churned up in the flood. The house lights come up, people around them scrape back their chairs and file out of the makeshift theatre and still she cries, until Paul folds her in his arms, his chest beneath hers teaching her to breathe, his sweater soaking up her tears. She is a bone-dry vessel slowly filling with cool, achingly clear water. Her breathing quiets as she leans against him, feeling his chest rise and fall, thrilling to the love of Jesus and the rhythmic stroking of Paul's hand gentle gentle on her hair.

Paul tells her she has been born again, brand new, and gives her a copy of the poem from the movie and a New Testament with all the things Jesus said printed in red. Over the next week she reads the four Gospels and struggles through "The Hound of Heaven," all five densely printed pages of it. Judy loves the romance of the beginning: "I fled Him, down the nights and down the days; I fled Him, down the arches of the years." Her favourite part, she tells Paul before her first Bible study meeting, is where the poet turns to Nature: "Let me greet you lip to lip, Let me twine with you caresses."

"But Judy," Paul half laughs, "he's supposed to move on from there. Only God can satisfy the soul."

"Well, that's the part I don't quite get. Why did God become flesh if He only meant to deal with the soul? And another thing, the God in this poem — He practically destroys the guy, strips him of everything just so he'll worship Him."

"'The Lord your God is a jealous God.' He must come first, Judy."

Judy nods, unconvinced. She's not all that crazy about this jealous God. He doesn't seem at all like Jesus in the Gospels, who was so kind to everyone — Mary and Martha, the adulterous woman, and especially Mary Magdalene. Judy imagines herself washing Christ's feet, kneading the callused soles, tracing the blue veins on his instep, drying them tenderly with her hair. Cradling them to her breast. She decides this is not something she should share with Paul just yet.

"You know the Bible pretty well, don't you?"

"I'm going to be a minister when I finish school."

"That must make your father happy." For the life of her Judy can't imagine why someone as good-looking as Paul would want to be a preacher.

Paul's smile twists. "Yeah, you'd think so. But he just keeps telling me, 'Many are called but few are chosen.' Typical."

Judy reaches over and touches his hand. "I think you'd make a great minister, Paul."

On the day of her baptism Judy kneels in front of the congregation, her bright hair encased in a plain white scarf, her dress the most sober thing she owns — still a mini, but at least navy and with white cuffs and collar. Pastor Leudy looks at her for a moment with searching eyes, as though he believes her new dress signifies only superficial change, but he baptizes her in the name of Jesus, who washes away the sins of the world. The baptismal water drying on her forehead, Judy kneels, eyes closed, while the congregation prays over her, welcoming her to the fold. As they sway around her, she breathes in the whisper scent of hair conditioner, whiff of aftershave, sharp accent of armpit, sweaty leather. They murmur words that sound as though they should make sense but don't. "That's speaking in tongues," Paul tells her as he walks her home. "It's a sign of God's grace. I should have told you about it. Were you scared?"

"Oh no," Judy says, not wanting to tell him she was more embarrassed than frightened. She doesn't want to spoil anything. Every time Paul smiles down at her with those eyes so blue and serious, she floods with gratitude, for without him she would still be trapped in her house with its slamming doors and screaming, and her own silent and unending litany of "You go to hell, you just go to hell." Without Paul she would still be sneaking off behind the 7-Eleven with anyone who would take her, drinking Slurpees spiked with rum and sleepily angling her chest to the hand shoving her bra up over her breast, her pelvis to the finger hiking up the panties caught in her crotch. Now she carries her reborn self like a shield. She has become a temple of the Lord, and those others cannot touch her. She tries periodically to tell Paul what exactly it is he has saved her from, but he always cuts her short with an awkward smile; "Judy, it's Jesus who has saved you. Jesus, not me."

On the day of her baptism, at her door, he holds out his arms to give her a hug. And in his arms she becomes liquid, moulding herself to every contour of his body, alive to his every stirring. She feels his body stiffen the slightest bit, and when she raises her lips to his sees his eyes widen with astonishment, and the briefest hesitation, before he lowers his lips to hers.

Judy sheds her other life like an old and dusty skin, barely speaking to Tabitha and the others, though she can feel the weight of their gaze upon her, mournful, resentful. When Paul asks whether Tabitha might like to come to a service or a film some evening, Judy hedges, never asks. Of all people it is Tabitha she must avoid. They are too much alike, know too much about one another, share too much of what Judy is trying to escape. Judy can't risk being dragged back. So she guards Jesus' love jealously even while she feels it shining from her pores, sparking from her fingertips.

She tells her parents she has been born again, and they smile into their tinkling glasses, but they seem relieved at her more subdued appearance. She is still out all the time, but now it's to Bible studies, church socials, which are boring for the most part but she goes because Paul goes. She joins the choir because Paul is in the choir, discovers she has a voice that soars above the others. So much so that Pastor Leudy has to ask her to tone it down a little. He does this politely enough; still, Judy knows he doesn't like her. But what does she care? She has the love of Jesus, and she's pretty sure she has Paul's love too. Though he seems oddly reluctant to show it, has not even tried to kiss her again.

After practice Judy idles through collecting her coat and

scarf, drops her music, gathers it slowly, lingers till only Paul is left in the choir loft, then asks if he will help her with a difficult alto passage. He sits at the organ, plays through her part. She leans in to examine the notation, swings her bright hair against his cheek, hears a sharp inhalation. Leans closer, brushing his shoulder with her breasts. His voice, strangled, says, "Judy, don't...," but his body turns to hers.

Paul's hands on her hips, lips at her mouth, tongue at her tongue. She shudders from so deep within herself that she cannot imagine ever finding a way back to the body she carries around with her every day. She moans and "Sshh, sshh," Paul murmurs into her mouth, fingers at her hair, at the nape of her neck, the shivers snaking to her breasts, while her whole body rises to him, pulses for him, for the rhythm of his tongue. And it is nothing like being with those others; no, this is pure, and blessed by Jesus, by a love so fiercely tender it opens her like a flower to his mouth and hands.

The next day Judy and Paul sit in the high school cafeteria and he says to her, "Judy, this is wrong. We have to stop."

"But Paul" — she reaches for his hand, which he hides under the table — "I don't understand. It's all just love, isn't it? I mean, that's supposed to be what it's all about. How can love be wrong?"

"It just is," he insists, and he sounds firm and knowledgeable, but he cannot raise his eyes to hers. This is a good sign.

That Sunday Pastor Leudy preaches from Saint Paul, who says that women must keep their hair covered in church. Their hair is their glory, and besides, it's distracting for men, who are head of the women as Christ is head of the Church.

"If your eye is sound, your whole body will be full of light; but if your eye is not sound, your whole body will be full of darkness. If then the light in you is darkness, how great is the darkness!" Pastor Leudy stares straight at Judy.

Judy decides she hasn't a lot of use for Saint Paul, or Pastor Leudy either. She may not know her Bible very well, but this feeling that rushes through her, for Jesus, for the Paul breathing beside her, is the holiest she has ever known. Pastor Leudy's eyes slide over her as though she is no longer there. Judy's spine tenses for battle. She takes stock of her weapons. Youth. Beauty. Love. She leans back in her pew and smiles full at Pastor Leudy.

Judy and Paul are straightening the room for tomorrow's Sunday school, not looking at one another, speaking in short bursts of instruction. Judy brushes Paul's shoulder stacking chairs, strokes his hand moving a table. Caresses the nape of his neck. "Bit of fluff," she says, and marvels at her voice, husky, and her power, stiffening Paul's entire body. She touches again. And he turns suddenly and grabs her so fiercely she cries out, laughing. They stretch out on the bare carpet, pressed to each other, length to length. And his fingers at her breasts, her neck, her thighs, lead her deep into slippery black folds that lap wild at heart, liver, womb, black-red and pulsing. With every new invasion, lips at a nipple, fingers at a zipper, she murmurs, moans, licks at the dark waves pouring through her, till she places his hand at her thighs, opens herself, peels back her darkness and welcomes him in. He cries out as he enters her, as if in pain.

Paul buries himself in her for a week. They make love anywhere they can be sure of even minimal privacy. In the bushes behind her house, in the church basement, in the park late at night. He tastes every part of her body, abandons himself to her flesh with mouth and hands until she is sure there is not one piece of her that does not bear his imprint.

Judy should be ecstatic. This is the culmination of all her hopes. She is ecstatic. But she would like to talk to Tabitha, the way they used to, about boys and how confusing they are. Paul becomes more frenzied each time they make love, the nips at her breast, her shoulder, her inner thighs driving her wild. But what Paul seems to be feeling isn't exactly passion. After that first time he has to masturbate himself to erection, eyes closed tight, face contorted. He pushes her hands away impatiently. And he says things like "Come, baby, come," not sounding like himself at all. Speaking to someone Judy doesn't recognize. "Paul," she falters, beginning to be fearful, "slow down, it's all right." Saturday night he can't bring himself to erection at all, and she holds him while he cries against her, while she says, "It's all right, Paul. It's all right." But she can't be sure that he hears her, that she is even there at all.

Judy tries to approach Tabitha, but she is always ringed with the wild things. One day, in desperation, Judy walks into the can at lunchtime.

"Look, girls," Tabitha says, staring at Judy with hurt and angry eyes, "she's wearing pink. Isn't that cute?" And she starts to sing "Like a Virgin" in a simpering voice to Judy's retreating back, the other wild things joining in chorus.

On Sunday Paul won't sit beside her in church. Pastor Leudy gives a sermon about what happens when two people have sex — he calls it intercourse. "They become one flesh," he says. Literally. It is a miracle, the moment when the profane becomes sacred, and that is why it must be so carefully guarded by the rites of marriage. If you have sex with someone you are not married to, and do not intend to marry, what happens to the parts of your flesh that became one? They are stranded, a piece of you irrevocably removed and trapped within alien flesh. Forever. And what happens to that bit of you if it is stranded in someone who will not be taken up in the rapture, will not see the resurrection of the body? How will you get your body back, whole and entire?

Judy looks up at Pastor Leudy, a stirring of fear in her chest. He looks back at her with calm eyes that seem to see into her very soul. She is the first to break their gaze, glances at Paul. He sits with his elbows propped on the pew in front of him, head dropped into his hands.

Judy doesn't see Paul for a week. He doesn't come to school, doesn't call, and she is afraid to call him at home, knowing that Pastor Leudy will be sure to get to the phone first.

On Sunday she dresses for church with special care: a cream-coloured miniskirt, pink shell sweater. Something neutral enough to appease Pastor Leudy, but revealing enough to remind Paul of all they have shared. If she can just see Paul, talk to him, touch him, he will be hers, she knows it. It has to be this way, because she can't go back. Paul has opened up feelings in her that she never thought possible. Because of him she has crossed a border she didn't even know was there, into a country that is uncharted and, without Paul, terrifying. She has become one of the girls the wild things coolly stare down when she goes to the bathroom. She cannot go back. And neither can Paul. She'll convince him.

She takes her seat in the middle of the church. Paul is already seated at the front, but she will find a way to approach him after the service. She pulls her skirt down over her thighs, picks up her hymnal. But there are no opening hymns, no announcements. Pastor Leudy stands and moves slowly to the front of the pulpit, spreads his hands, tall, dark, completely self-possessed. He motions to Paul, who comes forward and kneels before him.

"All that is dark shall be brought to light and all that is hidden shall be revealed." Pastor Leudy addresses the congregation over Paul's bent head, sorrowful, compassionate. He slips his fingers under Paul's chin, coaxes it upward. "What have you to confess, my son?"

Paul is mute. Judy hears the congregation begin to murmur around her, trees at the first breath of storm.

"My son, do not fear those who kill the body but cannot kill the soul; rather fear him who can destroy both soul and body in hell. Tell me." The congregation rises to its feet, a mighty wind of power and righteousness, *Yes Lord, amen.* Paul's tears trickle over Pastor Leudy's hand, still holding his chin. Judy hugs the pew with the back of her legs, cool wood on burning flesh.

Paul's throat convulses. "Last week," he begins dully, "I

committed the sin of lust." Judy feels the heat within her begin to drain away. "But I didn't know that's what it was, I
swear." Paul's face collapses against the back of the pastor's
hand, smearing it with tears and mucus. "I was only trying to
help her, to bring her to Jesus. But she wouldn't ... I couldn't
... but I know now, that's what it was. I know now. I'm sorry."

The pastor strokes the back of Paul's head with his other
hand. "Your faith has saved you, my son. Be at peace." He
straightens, looks out over the congregation. Fastens his eyes
on Judy.

"Is there another among you who needs to clear her soul
of its burden?"

If Paul would only look up at her, Judy would have the
strength to break free of the pastor's gaze, but Paul's eyes are
fixed on the floor.

"Come unto me, all that are heavy laden, and I will give
you rest."

The old hypocrite. Rest is the last thing he is offering. But
Judy is blunted, dulled, cannot find it within her to care, not
now when she knows she has lost Paul to something she never
understood. Lines from "The Hound of Heaven" sound
through her brain, something about tempting God's servants,
finding betrayal in their loyalty to God. She feels stupid for
not recognizing that there could be any conflict between loyalty to her and loyalty to God.

Pastor Leudy raises his arms and Judy feels the pull of his
power. The more he looks at her, the more heads turn in her
direction. She should leave, but to walk past all those pews in
defiance requires more courage than she's got, and besides,
she can't think where she would go. Certainly not to Tabitha,
whose friendship she trashed for what looks like complete
folly now. Judy rises, and the pressure of the congregation
propels her to the front of the church. She tries for the old
swing of the hips, ends up barely able to keep her knees from
trembling.

Judy stands in the centre of the room, under the pastor's
hand, under the dome of light, under the broad purple streamers that read, *His Banner over Me Is Love*. The faces of the congregation round white dots above a Joseph's coat of colour.

"Are you ready to make your confession, Judy?" Pastor Leudy asks.

Judy's mouth is sewn shut.

"Open your heart, child, there is no place to hide," says Pastor Leudy. *Amen, Lord*, murmurs the congregation, on its feet and swaying.

Pastor Leudy places his hands on Judy's shoulders, presses her to her knees. "Let us pray," he says, and the congregation moves to the front of the church, forming a circle of trousered and stockinged legs, cutting her off from Paul's kneeling body.

"Oh God, take this girl's heart and squeeze out its stubborn defiance" — *Yes Lord, yes*, the murmuring seals her ears — "take her unto You in your mercy and compassion, Lord" — *Amen*, they sigh — "take this girl and turn her from her evil ways, oh God" — *Illalla hellalla illallahe* — the congregation is moaning now, and beneath the sound Judy's silence, the only weapon she has left.

"She must receive the gift of tongues," the minister says. "If she cannot open her mouth on her own behalf, let the Holy Spirit speak through her, to protect her and us all from evil."

They pray, their hands above her a canopy of prayer, their voices beating about her ears, and now she wants desperately to speak, to put an end to it. She moves her tongue, probes the roof of her mouth, feels barren ridges, hollowed-out caverns.

"Lay her down on the floor," Pastor Leudy says. And hands take up her body and slide it to the floor, an arm brushing her breast, a hand bruising her thigh. She stares up at the dome of light while they pray over her again. Pastor Leudy kneels beside her, his eyes boring into hers. "Let her receive the laying on of hands." She closes her eyes tight then, but even so she knows his hands as they hover millimetres from her skin, follow every curve of ankle and knee, pelvis and breast. And he doesn't stop until he knows her — every hollow and rise that Paul has touched, kissed, entered. Pastor Leudy claims them all and, though he does not touch her, she feels him all the same, a charge between his body and hers, and she presses and presses her body into the hardwood but cannot escape. Her miniskirt has hiked up over one hip, her panties are exposed, she can feel the cold of the hardwood on her buttock. She sees herself as Pastor Leudy sees her. Let the floor open up and swallow her shame.

Pastor Leudy quells the prayers with one movement of his hand. "Enough," he says. "Leave her to her conscience and the voice of God."

The congregation leaves the room one by one. Pastor Leudy is last, and before he goes he stands over her and says, "There is a stubbornness, a resistance to the will of God in you, Judy. I saw it from the first. It is not just that you are sinful, it is that you revel in your sin. My son may have thought he wanted to help you closer to God but he was fooling himself. In you he saw his own weaknesses, his chief temptations. Like calls to like."

She turns her face to the floor and lies there a long while before she has the will to reach down and pull her skirt over her thighs.

Judy dumps the suitcase on the worn chenille bedspread, unzips its brand new vinyl lid, stares into its yawning mouth. Tomorrow she will go shopping and buy new jeans, sneakers, sweatshirts, T-shirts, bras, panties, socks. Everything new. She wanted an apartment no one had lived in before, but couldn't find one that came furnished and couldn't have afforded the rent anyway. So she's in a suite on the second floor of an old house in a rundown part of a town she doesn't know. The owners, Mr. and Mrs. Moog, live on the main floor, and their son is in the basement suite. "Just until he gets on his feet again," Mrs. Moog said, while Judy counted out the damage deposit. "He won't bother you." You bet he won't, Judy thought, if I have my way none of you will even see me. It seemed a bit odd to put your own son in the basement and a total stranger in the better rooms, but that was their business. Judy felt dirty and sticky from the long bus ride and wanted Mrs. Moog gone. She fended off all her questions, paid in cash and gave a fake name. Just in case. Though she can't imagine anyone coming after her.

She zips up the suitcase and shoves it into the closet, then runs a bath. The bathtub is a clawfoot, probably antique, chipped and water-stained but deep and long enough to lie back full length. At the sight of it Judy feels tears prick her eyes, undresses quickly and sits crouched in the tub while it fills, impatient to be completely covered with water.

The steaming water rises almost to the top of the tub and laps above her breasts. She leans back and sinks deeper, up to her neck, dribbles water from her fingers, watches the drops glitter against the light of the globe suspended from the ceiling, runs a finger down the stained sides of the old tub. Leaves a white streak through the grey. Ridges of dead skin years old edge the path her finger has left. She leaps from the bath in a surge of water, shivering. Throws towels on the pools forming on the linoleum, sponges herself off hurriedly, wraps a towel around herself, runs into the kitchen. Returns with sponges, Brillo pads, rubber gloves, Comet and Mr. Clean. Thanks God the former tenant left them under the sink, then remembers what she thinks of God. Flings Comet around the bathroom till she can barely see through the cloud, scrubs as though possessed, panting, muttering, choking on the cleaner-laden air. Blue and green foam eats at the grey stains, swishes down the drain to the squeak of orange rubber gloves and the scrape of metal pads against porcelain. By the time she is done there is not a mark on tub, sink or toilet, but she is too exhausted to bathe, just stumbles into the living room and slumps on the floor against the door, smelling of Mr. Clean and sweat.

Through the paint-bubbled wood comes a whisper: "Do you want to share a cigarette?" Judy doesn't answer. "They're American. Good ones. What do you say?" With trembling fingers she reaches up, slides the bolt into the lock. Looks up to the lamp in the centre of the ceiling, sees hundreds of hands clapping, raised towards the light.

Judy goes to the mall the next day. The Moogs' house is close to downtown and she walks past pawnshops and barbershops, a couple of bars and liquor stores, the fronts faded and dingy.

Some girls are standing on a corner, their hands stuffed in fake fur jackets, their legs disappearing into micro-minis. They flip their long hair and snap their gum and glance at Judy sullenly as she passes, but she keeps her head down and walks with her butt muscles tight.

At the mall she buys two sweatsuits, one grey, one navy, seven pairs of plain cotton briefs and two plain brassieres on sale. She wears one of the sweatsuits out of the store, leaving her skirt and sweater in the changing room. At the mall barbershop she gets her hair cut short, the blonde curls dull on the floor, the remaining hair hugging her head like a skullcap.

On the way back to the apartment she stops in at the corner grocer's, buys milk, bread, tomatoes, sausages. The clerk behind the till barely glances at her as he hands her the paper bag and her change. This is a good sign.

Back at the apartment, Judy runs her hands nervously over the stubble of her once glorious hair. Feels Paul's fingers tugging at the curls, his mouth tugging at her nipples. Is impaled on her longing. She had sneered at Pastor Leudy's sermon about the two becoming one flesh, but it turns out he was right about that too. She cannot lose the smell of Paul's flesh, the taste of his skin. His penis has carved out a place in her that cannot be filled. She stares, unseeing, out the window, until Mrs. Moog's son moves into focus. He is raking leaves. His lower lip props up a cigarette that he draws on deeply from time to time. He wears heavy-rimmed glasses that make it difficult to see his face, which is smudged with five o'clock shadow, making him look unwashed, unclean. He must think she has been watching him because he raises his head, pushes back the hat from his forehead and waves at her. He sees. Judy pulls back just as their eyes meet, just before Mrs. Moog calls out, "Get a move on with those leaves, and leave that girl alone now." It must have been him at her door last night. She imagines the stink of smoke as he leans towards her, feels again the whisper pierce the door. Sees dark hair and eyes and sharp white teeth, smells sweat and unwashed hair. Feels teeth at her breast, her thighs.

Judy goes into the bathroom and locks the door. Naked, she crouches on cold porcelain at a trickle of water from the faucet and scrubs herself red and raw with the stiff-bristled nail brush. Neck, arms, breasts, belly. Then she leans far back on her heels, positions the bristles between her thighs.

On Sunday she takes the sausages, cold and sweaty, from the fridge, takes the tomatoes from the basket by the window. They are sun-warmed and smooth, pliant as naked skin. She wants to kiss them to her nipples, crush them against her body, but instead she bends over the ache in her groin, pounding at her thigh until the feeling passes.

She slides the grill out of the oven drawer. It's caked with clumps of food charred past recognition, hard black lumps. In one of the lumps is a strand of singed blonde hair. Judy gags, carries the grill to the sink. Sees rust in the pipes, rotting food trapped in the drain.

"Hey," comes the whisper. "Why don't you open the door? We could play cards or something. Do you know blackjack?"

She runs water in the bath, as hot as it comes. Slides the grill into the water, watches the hair begin to loosen, the grease spots and flakes of charcoal rise to the surface. She returns to the kitchen, rummages among the cans and bottles under the sink. She is looking for anything with the emblem of a skeletal hand.

Judy picks up the phone and dials.

Tabitha's voice says, "Hello?... Hello?"

Judy opens her mouth but nothing comes out.

"Who is this? Richie, is that you?"

Tears edge up over Judy's eyelids and inch down her cheeks.

"I can hear breathing. Come on, Richie, quit kidding around." A long pause; then, hesitantly, "Judy? Is that you? Judy, your parents are frantic ..."

Judy hangs up the phone.

"I just want to bullshit, is that so bad? I just want to bullshit." Judy crouches by the door. "I can see you don't go out, and nobody comes in neither, and I figure that's got to get lonely. Hell, I know how that feels."

"Please go away," she mouths silently to the wood. "Please, leave me alone. I don't want to talk to you." She can hear him, he stays on the other side of the door a long time, breathing.

He's right about one thing. She is lonely. She's lonely with a shudder of cells that is beyond her control, that has nothing to do with mind or emotion. She raises the shirt of her sweatsuit, feels cool air on her nipples, rubs her palms over both breasts until her nipples rise and the ache swells at her thighs. She runs her hands over stomach and belly, feels Paul's lips, his teeth at the tender flesh. Her back arches, her thighs part. She slides her fingers down over her hips, her bristle of hair, slides into herself. She is silk, she is slick. She is aching. She hates, she hates him. She would fuck him senseless if he appeared in front of her. Her eyes close. She calls him up before her, his hair blond as hers, his eyes blue, not like hers but blue like angels. She sees his penis rise and reach for her, feels it nuzzle at her vulva. She sees his eyes widen as he cries out, she cries out. She pulses her fingers deeper, deeper, she is coming, she is ... the eyes of Pastor Leudy bore into hers. Her fingers are cold and lifeless inside her, sticky, glued together.

"Please open the door," Mrs. Moog's son whispers.

Judy twists out of herself, yanks her pants up, her top

down. Shakes on the floor in revulsion and something like surrender. He won't go away. He has found her out. Try as she may to hide under ugly sweats and ugly hair, he has caught her scent. He will never leave her alone.

"Please," he says, "I need help. I'm hurt and I can't see." He is almost sobbing. "Please. I'm blind."

Like speaks to like.

Judy opens the door and for the first time looks full in the face of Mrs. Moog's son. He is smaller than he seemed when she watched him from behind the curtain. Just barely as tall as Judy, and frail. The veins stand out on the hands that reach for her. He has a bruise over one eye and is straining for breath. My God, she thinks, he really has been hurt, and is snared by guilt.

"God damn muggers. They broke my glasses," he moans. "I'm blind without my glasses. Stone-blind. You've got to help me."

"It's all right, Mr. Moog," she says, "I'm here."

She takes the hand that gropes before her and leads him to the stairs.

"Maybe I should take you to your mother," she says, and he clutches at her arm.

"No," he says, "I'll be fine. Don't tell her. She gets upset."

But he is the one who appears upset. They begin the descent, he holding her hand tightly and clutching at her elbow, she trying to keep balance for them both.

At the door to his basement suite he says, "Please help me make some tea. I can't see where anything is. God damn muggers. Don't wake up my mother, she hates to see me like this. She worries too much. God damn muggers. Just a little slip, don't tell my mother." And she walks him into his flat. It is filthy. Dust on the tables, bedclothes a greying heap, sticky socks on the floor.

Judy goes into the kitchen to search for the tea and sees the bottles, piles of bottles — gin, beer, vodka. Sees gummy rings on the counters, a cockroach under the chair, and thinks, of course he's blind, blind drunk, and for about the thirty-thousandth time in her life she wonders why it is God decided to make her so stupid.

She turns her back on the squalid kitchen, walks into the other room, and for a man who was stumbling and nearly crying and having difficulty making his way down the stairs he's in pretty good spirits now, pulling out tooled leather wallets with plastic spirals sewn through eyelets at the edge and metal snaps to hold them shut. He makes them, he says, his words sewn together with a clumsy needle, his hands pawing the air. He's a good catch for a woman, he says, and she thinks, dear God, is she going to be a mark all the days of her life, and then realizes that's the first honest-to-God sincere prayer she's ever made.

"God damn muggers," he says, "took the only pair of glasses I got," and slyly puts his hand on the pair that lie on the battered dresser, slips them under the pillow as if Judy is the one who is blind.

"But I fought 'em off, yessir — got 'em back." He pulls them out from beneath the pillow and waves them in her face. "Black belt in...," and he chops the air with a blow that lands him flat on his ass on the sagging bed.

"... tell you a few things.... Show you a few, too...." His finger snakes forward, gnarled, tobacco-stained.

"How old do you think I am?" He staggers to his feet, swaying. "Old as sin." The bloodshot eye winks.

"Pleased a lot of women in my time." Hand advancing. "I knew the minute I saw you we had a lot in common," and she is shrinking, please God, shrinking into the wall, trying to make herself one with the dresser, the wall, anything but the living, breathing flesh that calls such demons to itself, and the hands trace out her body millimetres from contact, draw a line over thigh and hip, breast and belly, but this time they come too close and his face, his face leans in and there is no escape no matter how tight she closes her eyes, it is the face of evil and no confession will clear her no touch of human hands help her for the light that is in her is darkness, her mouth a hollow cavern, her tongue a frozen thing, help me, she prays to no one, help me. Beneath layers of clothing and skin something stirs, quivers, flexes. Licks deep into slippery black folds, laps warm at heart liver womb, black-red and pulsing, and up on its haunches howling, like the mighty wind carries all

before it rushes through gorge and windpipe rattles tonsils and loosens tongue. She opens her mouth, she speaks, eyes flaming at the strange and guttural sounds
         She Speaks

How to Talk to Plants

In the first place, be thankful you have a job. Any job. As the National Research Council officer said just before she turned you down for a grant to work on your thesis all summer, "Things are tough all over." Remember: you are making money. You will be able to return to university in the fall. In the second place....
      There is no second place.

On your first day, you shiver in Calgary's pre-dawn chill with half a dozen others and try to forget that Jefferson, who got you this job, is cosying up to your vacant pillow and, like the rest of the city, won't have to even think about getting up for another three hours. You are the lucky ones, your foreman tells you, the ones who made the cut. Your job is to tend the grounds of all the public board's schools. Prune trees, weed beds, spray herbicides and pesticides. The reason the spraying crew starts work so early, he says, is that, statistically, three a.m. is the time when Calgary winds are at their lowest. When you point out that it's also the time people are least likely to see workers in white plastic suits, with black goggles and masks strapped to their faces and huge packs strapped to their backs, spraying evil-smelling liquids onto playgrounds and schoolyards, nobody even cracks a smile. You feel radically out of place, transplanted into alien soil. But what the hell, it's only a summer job. You get in, do what you're told and get out with enough cash to see you through your degree. End of story.

Poke your feet, arms and head into white plastic. Elastic fastens onto the skin at ankle and wrist, snugs a neat circle encasing forehead, cheekbones, chin. Zip the zipper all the way up to lock the circle. Shove your feet into black rubber boots, your hands into yellow rubber gloves. Discover that even your fingers — rattling around in heavy gloves that cramp them into a permanent curl — even your fingers cannot breathe. Press the goggles and breathing mask to your face and adjust the elastic straps so that after a few minutes of minor exertion the mask seals itself to your skin with a ring of sweat, sucks onto your face like an octopus.

On your second day, or maybe third, your foreman comes up to you, maskless, hoodless, his suit open to the waist, and peers into your goggles, his mouth like a fish bumping the tank, his voice filtered through plastic, "This stuff is harmless — it's just Roundup. Babies can play in it right after their parents spray."

"Yeah, right," you mutter under your breath. "Ever hear of thalidomide? All this stuff is safe as houses until twenty years later, when the babies are born with flippers and the cancer blooms like a rose underground. No thank you." It doesn't really matter what you say. You're speaking into a plastic shell. A closed circuit.

"It's a pretty slack-ass job," Jefferson said when he told you he'd wangled it with his boss, slyly placing your application at the top of a huge pile of hopeful sheets of paper. Watching his supervisor leaf through them with his thumb before winking at Jeff and saying, "She looks the best qualified to me."

"I know, and I really appreciate it." You tried to put some enthusiasm in your voice. "But three a.m.... I'm not much of a morning person ..."

"It pays eighteen bucks an hour."

"... but what's a little loss of sleep?" You grinned and put on your very best Mae West growl. "Now come here and let me show you how grateful I am."

In the early days, before you and Jefferson started dating, before you started to see him as anything other than the guy who owned the condo next door, he came by unexpectedly as you were adding finishing touches to some Chili, and you asked him to stay for dinner. While you threw in the last dashes of cumin, chopped fresh coriander and minced jalapeños, he sat at the kitchen table, lifted down a sagging African violet from the window ledge and absently picked over the whole plant, gently removing wilted leaves and brown crusty petals, talking to you all the while about engineering and his own days in grad school. Under his tender hands the violet perked right up, positively preened, took on a deeper green, more blushing purple. And the violet's glow naturally transferred itself to Jefferson, so that you halted briefly in your ladling, and hunted through the fridge to snap off a sprig of parsley, to make the dish just that bit more festive.

While the jalapeños sang your tastebuds to life, he told you about some experiments he was trying, based on research in a book he'd been reading. He locked up some plants in one room, where he played Joy Division round the clock and sent them hate messages, YOU ARE UGLY AND USELESS, and he put others in a room with Bach and Vivaldi and sent them loving messages, *What a lovely shade of green you are, how fuzzy your leaves*.

"What happened?" you asked, reaching for his empty plate. He took your hand in his, pressed his lips to your wrist, and you felt the first tentative stirrings of desire, tender shoots probing, feeling their way.

The night of your first day on the job, he plants a kiss on your forehead, scoops his pants up from beside the bed and plucks a book from the back pocket.

"Here," he says. "Something to keep you occupied on breaks. It's a loan only, mind. A signed copy." He points at a smudge on the title page. You can't make out the signature, but the title of the book is *The Secret Life of Plants*.

Strap on your shoulder pack. Fully loaded, it weighs forty pounds. Remind yourself that you wanted to get some exercise this summer anyway. Do calculations of forty pounds multiplied by two hundred steps per hour over eight hours multiplied by calories burned. The hard plastic bumps all forty pounds hard against your kidneys, sloshes full of golden-brownish liquid. Try to shift the pack higher on your back. Think of something else. The straps that support the pack are leather and lined with sheepskin to keep them from digging into your shoulders too much, to prevent chafing. Remember: the people in charge are trying to make this as painless as possible.

Your first week on the job, your foreman has to point out which of the plants are weeds. Some of them sprout delicate green leaves, round or spear-shaped, and tiny flowers in purple or blue or sunny yellow. They look as if they'd make nice border plants. Not that weeds are determined by beauty. This is absolutely elementary botany, first-year stuff: Weed: n., a useless, bothersome, or noxious plant growing wild, esp. one that threatens the well-being of the desired crop. v., to root out, as from a flower bed, or to remove as inferior and undesirable (often followed by out): to weed out inept team members.

After one week you and Jefferson come up with your own definition: Weed: any plant tough enough to grow up through cracks in cement, so that impoverished students dressed like ill-equipped space persons have to spend hours walking across cement schoolyards spritzing intermittent splashes of green with Roundup.

For the first month, the most strenuous part of your workday turns out to be changing clothes. At three a.m., when the air is stiff with cold, you try to fit as many layers of kangaroo jacket and sweatshirt and T-shirt as possible under the white suit, and still you shiver. But by eight a.m. you are warming. You strip off the mask and goggles, peel down the suit to your waist and pull the kangaroo jacket over your head. Back into goggles and mask, zip up suit. By ten the sun is climbing the sky and you're sweltering. Out of goggles and mask, out of suit, tear off damp sweatshirt, suit up. It's like living in a sauna.

Your foreman turns out to have a love of conversation at any time of day, starting at three a.m., when you are groggy and grainy-eyed and still trying to figure out how you could drive twenty-five kilometres to the depot and not remember one gear or light change along the way. When he finds out that Jefferson is one of the engineers for the board and that you are doing graduate work in biology at the university, he tells you how he could have been an engineer but left school to do construction work during the boom and now here he is stranded in the bust with a $100,000 mortgage and a six-months-pregnant wife. While you sit in the truck with the blue school-board logo on the door and eat your McDonald's McMuffin or your Robin's doughnut from sticky wax paper, drink coffee from your steel Thermos, you stare out the window into a murky dawn and answer in monosyllables. You realize that calling yourself not-a-morning-person can't even come close to describing the rawness of physical pain your body experiences at this hour, the saw-edge scrape of his words on your ear.

Every once in a while he pulls into a 7-Eleven and calls home. In these periods of silent reprieve you snatch up the book Jeff gave you and read in huge gulps.

In the first chapter, a scientist is sitting beside his philodendron when he whimsically decides to hook up electrodes to one of its leaves, the little suction cups sealed to the leaf by agar jelly and connected by a wire to a machine like a lie detector, one that measures emotional response through changes in electrical current. In an effort to discover a way of raising such a response in the plant, he dunks one of the leaves in a cup of hot coffee, this being all he has to hand. Nothing. But of course, hot coffee isn't that big a threat. So he decides he'll get a match and burn the leaf.

The needle flies all over the page before he even reaches for the match. It looks as though the plant is reading his mind.

Swing round the long plastic tube that ends in a metal rod with a handle like a gun. Spritz a couple of times to clear the line and watch the brownish liquid run along the tube like an IV. Put the end of the nozzle close to the plant, where its temple would be if it had one. Pull the trigger. Spritz.

On good days, when the wind is too high for spraying but there's no rain, you pinch pines. When your foreman first tells you this is what you'll be doing, you try to come up with the nudge-nudge kind of response that seems called for. Point me at those pines, you say with a feeble attempt at a Groucho cigar pull, and I'll pinch 'em till they're blue spruce. Ha, ha, says your foreman, and shows you how to trim back the tender young shoots, spongy with new growth that throbs a brilliant, hopeful green. First you wrap your fingers firmly around the base of the shoot, just out of reach of the mature, sharp needles. The stubs of the potential needles, needles barely born, nuzzle bumpy and soft under your hand. Grasping the middle of the shoot with the other hand, you snap down and around in one twist of the wrist. Sap beads up in scores of glistening drops over the surface of the wound. You brush them away with one finger and turn quickly to the next one, before the beads well up again.

You do this so the tree won't grow too high or too wide for its bed, won't overshadow the flowers at its base, won't block the sunlight from the windows it fronts. It crosses your mind to wonder why the grounds people are planting trees that normally grow to heights of fifteen to twenty feet as border plants. But you don't say anything.

Even on bad days, when you are spraying from the huge tanker truck, hanging on for dear life while your foreman drives at a forty-five-degree angle along a slope and it's all you can do to keep the flow going, never mind whether it's steady, even on these days you are thankful you're not on gopher detail. What with budget cutbacks and Humane Society complaints about agonizing deaths from strychnine, the crew have been instructed to block all the holes but two, pour water down one hole and bash the gophers over the head with a shovel as they try to escape out the other. You have to change your way of thinking, Jefferson says, or it'll drive you crazy. Don't think of gophers as cute little animals who stand up to sniff the air and sometimes eat out of your hand. They are rodents, pests. Children turn ankles in the holes they leave behind in parks and schoolyards. Besides, why should you feel guilty? Motorists kill thousands every year.

Time your spraying so you're ready to leave before the gopher crew starts in the morning. If this fails, try to ignore the shouts of triumph that follow each dull metallic ring. Above all, if the foreman of the gopher crew wanders over to talk to your foreman before you leave for the day, avoid making any comment about the gopher tails hanging from the brim of his Blue Jays baseball cap. Rodent, you will want to say to him, feeling your head swelling like some ever more empty gourd, the small kernels of ever more useless knowledge rattling around it like drying rat turds. Rodent: belonging to the order Rodentia, which is composed of the gnawing mammals, including squirrels, mice and beavers. The fucking symbol of Canada is a goddamn rodent, you will want to yell at his hat.

But you won't.

In mid-June you stand in front of your hoya with a mineral-encrusted watering can, staring at its spiky stem and dusty leaves. You were never overly attentive to your plants, certainly never talked to them as the author of *The Secret Life* suggests, considering the idea flaky. But you used to water them every Saturday morning, until your mornings got eaten up by your job. Maybe you should have sent them encouraging messages. The scientist claims that houseplants can last almost indefinitely in the absence of water and other nutrients if only they sense compassionate thought directed their way. You hold the hoya above the garbage can, trying to convince yourself that it is somehow more excusable to kill something by neglect than by design. Trying to think what on earth you could have said, if you'd ever thought to send it telepathic messages. Briefly you consider burying it in the back yard, then give your head a shake and dump it in the trash. Your eyes are burning. You really must get more sleep or you'll end up as big a flake as the scientist.

Excited and amazed by his recent experiments, and determined to prove that plants can not only read human minds but also communicate, the scientist hires five grad students for another experiment. First they draw lots. Then they disperse. The chosen one returns to the lab at a time known only to him, enters a room containing only two plants and proceeds to rip one of them to shreds in front of the other. No human, not even the scientist, knows the identity of the murderer. Only the surviving plant knows. When the students are marched by, it identifies the killer. Sends tiny electrical impulses of pure pain and panic into the electrodes suctioned to its skin.

Try to find a time when you can sleep. Go to bed as soon as you get home, eleven o'clock. The brightest time of the day. Pull the blinds tight, pull the blankets over your head, pull the chenille threads from the bedspread. Count sheep. Watch them turn to gophers as they leap over the stile, dropping like stones as they run smack into the steel shovel. Get up. Make coffee, as if you need more caffeine. Look out the window at the dandelions at the back of your condo. The fluffy heads you used to blow wishes on now look dusty and grey. Unsanitary. Make lunch or brunch or dinner or supper. Watch a game show and then a couple of soaps. If you can get to sleep by three p.m., you may be able to stay awake four hours later, when Jefferson calls. Go to bed. Three p.m., the hottest time of the day.

Every morning your foreman slams into the driver's seat beside you, takes a big slurp from his 7-Eleven paper cup and flips on CKXL, The Classic Rock Station. Even in the later hours of the morning, when the show is called "Light Favourites," the DJs scream their information, sounding like one continuous commercial. Your toes and fingers curl but you try to keep your lip from doing likewise. You don't want to look like a snob. "The US faces increasing pressure to once more take up arms against Iraq. Saddam Hussein has again refused to comply with the terms of the cease-fire agreement and allow UN inspectors to monitor his stockpile of weapons. There is suspicion that he has massive reserves of chemical and biological weaponry, of the kind that he has used on the Kurds in the past, and that he may be planning another offensive."

"Christ," says your foreman, "that man's a waste of space. We should've taken him out when we had the chance."

You open your mouth to comment, but he says, "Wait, wait — I want to hear this." And he turns up the volume.

Spend all your waking hours, outside of those consumed by your job, in front of the TV. Toy with the idea of becoming a professional soap watcher, whose job is to keep the storylines straight and to warn "Another World" that the serial killer they thought was dead is really on "General Hospital," posing as a doctor. Start taping the late-

afternoon soaps so you can watch them in the morning instead of game shows. Try to remember the title of your thesis. To remember why you ever thought you wanted to do it in the first place. Phone your supervisor to see if he can remind you, and start a chain of voice-mail circuitry that loops back on itself over and over and never arrives at a living, breathing human voice. Scan the papers every day for signs of rain. Herbicide doesn't adhere when it rains. Spend your nights praying for rain, even though you know deep in your stomach that this will be one of the driest summers on record.

In July the temperatures rise to the mid-80s by nine a.m. You strip down until all you are wearing under your plastic suit is a tank top and a minuscule pair of shorts, and still your suit reaches internal temps of 120, tugs at your skin like a leech. You spend hours breathing the smell of your sweat and breath and, though you get used to the smell, you cannot get used to your own secretions, the way they line your lip, trickle down your jaw. This is an intimacy you didn't bargain on, this closeness to yourself. Your foreman and the rest of the crew look comfortable and are getting a great tan wearing shorts and rubber boots, the women in bikini tops, the men bared-chested or in cotton shirts open to the waist. Laughing, talking. Breathing in poison. Every so often they glance at you and shake their heads.

Try to get away on weekends, go camping, perhaps. To get away from the phone that never rings because no one knows when you might be trying to sleep. To spend time with the boyfriend you never see, maybe have sex now that you are both awake at the same time and in the same place. Discover that now, miraculously, you can sleep. In the middle of conversations. In the middle of foreplay. Flinch when he touches the purplish-green bruises on your shoulders, left by the sheepskin-lined straps; flinch as though they are scars.

In the morning you stand at the door of the trailer, suck in the smells of bacon frying and coffee perking in chill mountain air, gaze out on deciduous and coniferous trees and moss and undergrowth and realize that you are in a place without weeds. Undifferentiated growth — the unexpected pleasure of it scrapes you raw, brings you close to tears. You can almost hear the hiss of cool, moist air being released from their stomata — their exhale, your inhale. You are breathing through every pore of your skin. Almost reluctantly you turn to Jefferson.

"I'm sorry about last night." You reach to touch his shoulder with one hesitant finger, then change your mind.

He looks up from the sizzling bacon. "No sweat," he says. "I know you're getting all turned around with this schedule." He hands you a steaming coffee.

"I feel like the subject of some weird experiment myself," you say, with a nervous laugh that grates on your ears.

"What?" He laughs and turns back to flip the eggs. One breaks against the cast-iron rim and leaks a sickly yellow.

"Oh, I don't know. Like some kind of sleep deprivation study." Your tongue feels dusty, out of the habit of conversation. "Never mind. Forget it."

Jeff keeps the broken egg for himself, makes you a present of the complete egg and bacon fried crisp the way you like it. But the soft yolk clogs your tastebuds, and after one bite you set the plate aside.

After breakfast you and Jefferson go for a walk. You would like to hold his hand, lean into his shoulder, rub his wool sweater with your cheek. But then you see it. A dandelion, or what's left of it this late in the season. The head has blown away, the stalk has shrivelled, all that's left is the jagged leaves, tortured and crawling.

You stop dead in your tracks.

"I want to go back."

Jeff stares at you. "What?"

"I want to go back now."

"But we just got here. What's wrong?"

"Nothing," you snap. He must be able to see your hands shaking, your whole body vibrating. "Nothing," you say. And wait for him to pull it out of you, hold you in spite of yourself, stroke you with tender hands till your trembling ceases.

He does nothing.

You tramp back to camp, needles wincing under your feet, and pack up without speaking. On the way home you hunch against the window, your shoulder turned against him, tears beading on your cheeks. You wipe them away and still they rise.

Monday morning. You drag yourself to the Toyota, throw your Thermos on the seat and sit for a moment with forehead pressed to the steering wheel, warm blood pulsing against cold plastic. What you need is Handel's *Water Music*, or Bach's Brandenburg Concertos, a world of order and harmony. But above all you need to stay awake, so you turn on the radio and ignition simultaneously and edge onto the empty street to the blare of some rap artist telling you women are lying, cheating, cruel bitches who deserve to be put in their place.

As you pull into the depot, a few lonely stars not blotted out by the city's glare pulse down on you, an unreadable Morse code. You enter the quonset to pick up your gear, and find your foreman already there, watching television in the staff area.

"I'll just be a minute," he says over his shoulder. "They're running a retrospective on the Gulf War. I bet things are heating up again."

On the TV, two young men with crew cuts and white shirts watch their own screen, their hands on a keyboard below it. A pale blue cross framed by pale blue corners floats over buildings that are seen from a long distance. The picture is murky, almost sepia in colour and effect. The cross hovers over one of the buildings and beneath it the building blooms into a silent explosion of flame and cloud. The young men cheer and clap each other on the back. Your foreman smacks his fist into his other hand. "Yes!" he mutters.

Alone in the school-board truck, you flick on the overhead light and start to read.

The scientist has discovered through further experimentation that his plants become distressed at the death of even the smallest microbes. Yogurt that kills bacteria in the throat as it is swallowed causes vegetable turmoil; hot water poured down a drain, slaughtering millions of living things unseen by the human eye, sends the electromagnetic needle clawing frantically at the page. He decides that perhaps there is a consciousness of life at the cellular level, life that recognizes and responds to other life. To test this theory, he sets up a machine that randomly dumps live shrimp into boiling water to see if the plants can sense this carnage as it's happening.

In early August you stand in your kitchen and try to focus bleary eyes on the letter from the Research Council. It is a wordier version of the earlier telephone kiss-off, with one interesting addition. Your supervisor didn't give you a recommendation. You have to read this several times before it sinks in. He was the one who helped you apply. This makes no sense. But they send quotes from his damning letter of unrecommendation. "Good at following instructions," you read, and the text fragments before your eyes; "not enough initiative to work unsupervised." You see the hours and hours you worked on his research project, staining the slides, poring over them through the microscope. The hours you spent thinking you were building up a bank of goodwill that would pay out huge dividends at just such a time. The hours you put in because you were too weak to say you needed more time on your own work, because you would not stand up to the man in the white coat, who surely had only your best interests at heart. No wonder he hasn't returned your calls.

"So," you say to Jefferson, who is sitting beside you on the couch, "how did the experiment go in the end?" You have stayed awake from eleven a.m. to six p.m., determined to finally confront him. He has barely had time to sit down.

"The experiment? What experiment?"

"With the plants. In the separate rooms. The one based on this book." You wave it at him. "How did it turn out?"

"Well, they died."

"Both sets?"

"Yeah, but it doesn't mean the experiment failed. You and I got involved and this new project at work was taking up a lot of time and I forgot to keep the messages going. It wasn't that big a deal."

He puts his hand on your knee. "Now, what shall we do with the evening? Are you hungry?"

"It's not scientific, you know," you say belligerently.

He stares at you for a moment, then says, "Well, no, not really. But you have to admit it's a pretty neat idea, that we might actually be able to talk to plants, or at least read their reactions. Now come on, daylight's burning and we don't want to waste it."

"It's not science, just some kind of New Age hocus-pocus. I can't believe you wasted your time on it." You jab your finger at the top corner of the back cover. "See? It's not even listed under science. *Occult, New Age.* It's not even science."

"Who *cares*?" His voice rises but he reins it in and ends quietly, "I just don't know what's gotten into you lately." He heads for the kitchen, and you stare after him, dangling from one hand the book you've been waving at him like a weapon.

Now the scientist is trying to figure out how much of the plant needs to be around to telepathically register the fact of death. With a razor he shreds the leaves, slicing them into smaller and smaller bits, until eventually he is left with a small circle of green matter just the size of the suction cup electrode. With some reluctance, after he has rigged up the patch of leaf to the machine, he lights a match and, ignoring the needle scratching madly at the page, begins to burn the leaf, cell by sensitive cell.

You close the book, and your eyes, sit with the book in your lap and wonder what happened to the student who murdered the plant, the killer who was psychically fingered by the survivor. What happened to his cells? Did they shudder with the knowledge of what the body as a whole was doing? The scientist dismisses this possibility easily, excusing the student and himself because they acted only in the interests of science, which noble purpose absolves them of guilt. But you are not at all sure on this point. And you need to be sure, because if plants truly are sentient beings, if cells truly do pulse with awareness of all life, what kind of judgements are they levelling against a species whose only understanding of how to measure life is to kill it?

What are they saying about you?

Will your hands to stillness, control. Slowly and with total concentration, tear out each leaf of the book and shred it in long, careful strips. In the fireplace, layer the strips in rows of five, another row crosswise, another crosswise again, the way you saw Jefferson make the fire in the mountains. Strike the match and hold it till the flame is full and yellow, then hold the flame to the paper piled on the grate. Watch the flames curl and blacken each separate strip.

When Jeff comes back from the kitchen with the coffee he made in an effort to calm down and salvage something of the evening, it takes him a minute to realize what's making such a tidy little bonfire.

"I cannot believe you'd do something like this," he yells, clutching what's left of his book in hands black with ashes. "What the hell were you thinking of?"

"What I can't believe is that you could even read such a book, let alone do these experiments. The man's a sadist."

"Jesus Christ, they're just *plants*!"

"He thought they were alive, Jeff, really alive. He thought every single cell was aware of the difference between life and death."

"It was just an experiment ..."

"That's not the point," you stammer.

"This is an insane conversation, do you know that?" Jeff is stomping around the room now, waving his blackened hands. "Do you want to know the point? Do you?" He strides up close and shoves his head into your face, "You're the one doing the killing, not me!" He stops and smacks his head with his flattened hand, leaving a black smudge on his forehead. "I cannot believe I actually said that. Do you see how crazy this is?"

His mouth opens and closes, opens and closes. The space between you is so dead that you have to fight the impulse to raise your fingers to see if they'll bump against a pane of glass.

This reminds you of something, something that's been at the back of your head all along. An experiment. In the sixties, maybe. A group of carefully selected volunteers. You are very important people, they were probably told, you are the ones who made the cut. And then they were led into a room with a two-way mirror. You can see out, they were told, but no one can see in. This was an important part of the experiment, that no one could see in. In the other room was a human being strapped into a chair, little rubber suction cups attached to his skull with agar jelly. The subjects of the experiment were led to a panel with a dial switch and a meter that recorded voltage. The person in that room holds vital information, they were told, but he has to be encouraged to reveal it. All you have to do is turn the switch to administer an electric shock. We will take full responsibility. Remember that. Now, turn the dial.

Pulses of electricity ran along the wires to the man's skull, studded with suction cups. The man writhed and screamed and twisted in his bonds, but didn't divulge the information. Turn up the voltage, the subjects were told. And they did. The needle quivering into the danger zone, they must have wondered just what the man was supposed to disclose, but they didn't say anything. It was a little more difficult to convince them to twist the dial when they could hear the man's screams; they protested more then. But still, in the end, they did as they were told.

And the scientists were amazed. They made analogies to Hitler's Germany. They published in every major psychological journal. The experiment became a classic of its kind, which is probably why you know of it, since psychology is not your field.

The scientists offered the men psychological counselling after they were told what part they had actually played. After they were told that, absolved of all responsibility, they had administered enough voltage to kill the man strapped to the chair. Lucky for him that it was all a fake, that the man was an actor. But of course the subjects didn't know that at the time.

You don't remember if the scientists did any follow-up on the subjects in the weeks, months, years after the experiment was concluded. After the subjects had confronted what they were capable of. Regardless of the cushion of counselling, in spite of every effort to make their recovery as painless as possible, that kind of experience must leave its mark. Lesions on the brain, sore spots you'd return to again and again, no matter how you flinched when you touched them.

You hear a door slam as if from miles away. Jefferson is gone.

You're late. The sun is already in the sky when you leave for work, but you woke so often to check for Jefferson that you slept far beyond the alarm. You walk across the open field towards the spraying truck, clumsy in your rubber boots, your plastic thighs swishing together, thankful that your mask hides your swollen eyes and puffy face. The gopher crew are on coffee break, lolling up against their truck, which is parked a short distance from the spraying truck. Too far for you to see their kill piled on the tailgate, for which you are grateful.

Your foreman calls, "Wind's up today. We'll be on gopher detail. You can get out of that gear." You nod at him and head to the back of the truck to change. He and the others seem to be watching you closely, tensely.

You duck your head and start for the passenger door. Stop. Something is sitting on the hood of the truck. Something grey-ish brown at the top and reddish at the bottom. A gopher. A gopher with a bashed-in skull dripping blood sluggishly onto the hood. You walk around to look more closely. The gopher sits hunched over like a paunchy old man, his belly soft and exposed, his paws curled up and spread open as if in a gesture of bewilderment. Someone has tied the gopher to the hood ornament with a piece of string and its own tail, which has been broken in several places in the attempt, and the bones poke through the sparse tail hair like tiny white needles.

You head out into the fields without a backward glance.

"Hey!" yells your foreman. "Come back! We were just pulling your leg!"

Look out over a field in which all you can see is weeds. Inside your suit, feel the heat set up a shudder in your chest, a thousand wings beating, beating. Feel your mouth suck in air rank with sweat and black rubber, your lungs pull back from air's entry, cells shrinking, thudding up against the inescapable bone of your spine. Quick. Think about something else. Try to think yourself into the future, back at grad school, poring over stained cross-sections. Becoming a scientist. Think about the scientist who wanted to talk to plants, an idiot who asked the wrong questions and then didn't listen for the answers. You could have told him that the challenge is not how to talk to plants, but how to get them to shut up. They whisper things you'd rather not hear. Sucker, they whisper, n., a shoot from an underground root or stem; a person too easily deceived, too readily imposed upon. Perhaps it is better to ask the wrong questions, they whisper, than to ask no questions at all.

Shuck off the plastic suit. Tear away the mask. Realize that, above all, you can no longer afford to be a closed circuit behind a plastic case that lets you see out but lets no one see in. Feel the breeze lick the sweat from your body. The air is sifted through with poison but no matter. This is the world you live in. Peel off damp T-shirt and shorts. Lie flat on the patch of gravel beneath you, your head by the sole remaining dandelion. Feel each sharp and rounded contact point, cold hard stones poking into soft and yielding skin. Feel your fingers, toes, nipples, every cell of your body stretching for contact, probing the soil, lengthening into tender shoots feeling their way around each tiny rock, each scrap of soil, through plant matter, animal refuse. Put your ear close to the weed's head, where its mouth would be if it had one. Lie very still.

A Fragile Thaw

We stand in the park, Martin and I, facing away from each other. Above us a broad band of chinook cloud looms a deep blue, like a beautiful but dangerous bird about to settle over its brood for the night, and beyond it, to the west, a glorious red sunset streaks the horizon, searing the clouds with gold. Some kids dragging their sleds up a distant ridge complete what could be a Norman Rockwell Christmas card. Overdrawn, sentimental, too brightly coloured for my taste. Just the kind of card I used to send out every year.

The chinook blew in earlier this afternoon, not strong enough to melt the snow, but enough to take the bitterness out of the chill. As soon as my mother made a move for the turkey, which was thawing in cold water in the sink, Martin suggested we rent a Christmas video before they got too picked over. So we buttoned and booted and suited up and left my mother cursing the turkey, which was not thawing fast enough.

"I don't know why this happens every year," she muttered sourly, poking at the pebbly skin. "All you have to do is follow the *Joy of Cooking* guidelines." My cue to take up arms for the traditional Christmas turkey fight, to say, as I usually do, that I did follow the directions, to the letter, but the authors obviously have rocks in their head when it comes to turkeys, because no matter how faithfully you stick to their instructions you still end up wrestling icy innards from a frozen cavity. Martin's cue to step between us, to steer me to the door before I say something we all regret. Except that this time, as far as I'm concerned, the bird can stay frozen into the new year.

I turn towards the sunset, into wind that pushes the breath back into my throat. "You go on," I say. "I'd like to stay here and watch the sunset. Would you mind?" Knowing he can't very well say anything but "No, of course I don't mind, Lily." Not this Christmas.

"What do you want me to get?" he asks.

"Oh, anything." And he shoots me the surreptitious look he so often shoots at me these days. Then lopes off towards the store, his long strides and body loose beneath bulky clothing almost enough to crack my heart.

Almost but not quite. I am tensile steel that blunts any gesture of kindness or concern. I am cold as wrought iron that seals itself to skin, rips unmercifully when tentative fingers pull back from such savage chill.

My father and mother flew in for Christmas on the twenty-second, as they do every year. Martin brought them back from the airport. My mother, face grey beneath impeccable makeup, took one look at me and rushed forward — "Oh, darling" — arms out. I took her gingerly by the shoulders, bent down to peck at her cheek. She stiffened, then handed me her navy handbag and red silk scarf and headed for the bathroom off the foyer.

"She threw up on the plane," my father told me with stiff jollity, surrendering his duffel coat to Martin. Martin handed it to Melanie, who held it in her arms as though it were a living thing. The taps burst on behind the bathroom door. "All these years she's never been airsick and suddenly — boom. Sick as a dog." He dropped his voice. "Well, she's been pretty het up about coming out this year. Hard on everyone, really." His face flushed, eyes blurred. He smelled of Scotch.

"Melanie," I said, more sharply than I intended, "hang up your grandfather's coat."

The bathroom door swung open, revealing my mother scrubbing at the sleeve of her navy winter coat. "I was not sick as a dog, George. I was hardly sick at all."

"Don't know why she didn't just use the airsick bag," Dad continued at full volume. "That's what it's there for. But no, she has to try to make it to the bathroom, down a tiny aisle in the middle of turbulence, and, sure enough, she's sick all over herself. Here, chicken," he said to Melanie, who was fumbling to hook the heavy coat over a wooden hanger, "let me help."

The taps shut off and my mother emerged and handed her coat to Martin with a delicate shudder. "Don't be disgusting, George. Besides, it was only my sleeve." She paused in front of the hall mirror and patted herself into order. "I'm fine, dear," she said to me, not waiting to be asked. "You know how your father loves to fuss."

"I could do with a Scotch," Dad said, with a hopeful look towards Martin.

"You had two on the plane, George. That's two more than you usually have and the flight's only an hour long. Tea will be fine, dear."

"Remember Christmas a few years back?" My father has always launched into storytelling when faced with difficult situations. "Brenda was what — fourteen? And some friend of yours brought champagne over on Christmas Eve."

I flinched, and my mother cast a nervous glance in my direction. "Hush now, George."

"Are you telling me we can't even mention her name?" my father blustered. He's one of those people who, when you say you've heard this one before, still push through to the bitter end. "Funniest thing I ever saw, Brenda all woozy and white as a sheet, draped over the toilet, with Melanie slouched on the floor beside her, laughing and scrubbing at Brenda's face with a wet dishcloth. Brenda'd been giving her sips too, the monkey. And then those Mormon students of yours dropped by, Martin, with a present from the class — a wreath or something, I forget. And Brenda was moaning, 'Don't let them see me, Mom,' so you stood there, Lily, you and Martin, like sentries. Funniest thing I ever saw, those kids trying to peek round the door, hoping for a cup of hot chocolate or something. It was wickedly cold outside, but you wouldn't even let them past the porch. You were only wearing a light sweater, Lily, and you were damn near blue by the time they finally left. Funniest thing I ever saw." Dad faltered to the end, eyes wet, bluff called. He seemed to have shrunk since I had last seen him. With the bluster of his story deflated, he was an old man in clothes too big. We stood silent for a moment, like chess pieces on the large squares of black and white tile. Martin moved towards me. I moved away.

My mother, who can always be counted on to throw herself into the breach, said, "What's that quote you like so much, Martin? Something about loose liquor?" Her laugh shivered the foyer.

"Liquor talk mighty loud when it get loose from the jug," Martin said, half smiling and placing a hand on Melanie's shoulder. Her hand crept up to his.

"Yes, well. You might just take a page from that book, George," my mother said. Dad turned and shambled towards the family room. "And George," she called to his back, "take out that box of tarts from my suitcase so Lily can put them straight in the freezer. They shouldn't have had time to thaw on the plane."

"Yes, my little commandant," my father said to her, with a wink at Melanie as he headed for the suitcases.

"Mincemeat tarts for Christmas Eve," my mother said to me, then smiled at Melanie. "Now you be sure to leave them there, none of your raiding."

Melanie smiled. A very small smile. She hasn't stolen a single one of the tarts or cookies or bourbon balls that friends have stocked our freezer with this year. I've been checking.

The chinook's picking up. Gusts up to sixty miles per hour, the forecast said. Strong enough and dry enough to evaporate ice without melting it. "Sublimation, it's called," Melanie told me the other night, offering the information with an apologetic swing of her bangs. "The wind sort of steals the molecules right off the ice." She's quite keen on science, has a huge crush on her teacher. She certainly spends whatever time she can volunteering for class projects after school. "Don't slouch, Melanie," I said, and watched her face seal itself off from me.

I close my eyes, the sear of clouds etched on my lids, and breathe in sunset as though I could suck in its heat and light and store them in my innermost core. She is all bones and angles, Melanie. "You need fattening up, dear," my mother said to her this morning.

"I do feed her, Mother," I said. It's just that Melanie's at that awkward age — eleven — when her whole body is concentrated on what's going on beneath the surface, using every spare bit of energy for the leap into puberty. Preparations for a monthly flow, the dropping of labia, the nudging outwards of breast. Her body doesn't fit itself. It bangs and stumbles and bruises. Brenda was just the same at that age, gangly, painfully awkward. Then the sudden rounding into beauty.

I flap my arms and stamp my feet to shake feeling back into my limbs. I'd like to sit on the bench beside the swings, but my jacket is short and the wood is cold. Perhaps I could try swinging to keep my blood flow up; watch the kids play in the snow, drag their sleds to the top of a distant ridge, scream hysterically as they plunge down the slope. At least somebody's doing something that fits the season.

Last night my mother made dinner. Pork pot roast and vegetables, mincemeat–apple crisp. We ate in silence except for requests for salt, applesauce. Tinkle of Waterford, ring of sterling on china. All very polite. The Norman Rockwell family before Christmas. Grandma, Grandpa, Mom and Pop and daughter. No empty chair to mark an absence. The wounded family suturing itself with remarks on the tender flesh of pork.

"Very nice dinner, Carol."

"Thank you, Martin."

My throat closed like a fist.

"I found a Christmas story, Mom," Melanie's voice rose tentative at my elbow. "We talked about it in school today. It's from *Goodbye to All That*, by Robert Graves."

"It's from what?" My father helped himself to another spoonful of gravy.

"*Goodbye to All That*. A book he wrote about the First World War." Melanie twisted her fingers round the stem of her glass, and knocked it against her plate. Brenda once raised her glass in a toast and hit the top of the decanter with such force that the base of her glass snapped clean off the stem and whizzed across the table like a discus.

Eyes back on my plate, I moved mashed potatoes away from the grey slab of pork, pushed carrots apart from celery. Clumps of food lined up around the edges, empty space in the centre.

"It's even a true story," Melanie said.

"Really, honey?" My mother's voice too bright. "It sounds lovely. Why don't you tell it to us?"

Melanie glanced at me. "Well, he says one Christmas Eve during the war, the soldiers ceased fire and then all by themselves they wandered into — what's that space between the war lines?"

"No man's land," Martin said, laying down his knife and fork to give her his full attention.

"Right, no man's land." Her voice perked up under Martin's encouraging smile. "Anyway, they all went there and shared cigarettes and played cards and talked all Christmas Day. Isn't that neat?"

"And then I suppose they went back to blasting one another to pieces Boxing Day?" The words were out before I realized it.

"Lily," Martin hissed. I looked defiantly round the table. No one would meet my eyes.

"It's a lovely story, honey," he said. Melanie smiled, blinking rapidly.

"Well," my mother said, "I hope everyone saved room for apple crisp and ice cream." She started to remove plates while I mashed my carrots to a pulp.

"That's OK, Carol," Martin said firmly. "Lily and I will clear." And he dumped his plate on top of mine.

When we got into the kitchen, he dropped our best china

on the counter as though it were Corelle Living Ware and he were testing it for durability. He stood with his back to me and said, trying for no expression, "I know this is hard for you, Lily, but try to remember it's hard for all of us. You're not the only one in pain here. You are not the only one. Take it out on me as much as you like, but cut Melanie some slack. You have another daughter, you know. You cut her some slack."

I turned on the taps full force and squirted too much soap into the sink, keeping my eyes on the bubbles foaming up from the spray. I knew without looking at him that the veins at the back of his neck were raised and pulsing, flushing his neck an angry red. His fists white and bunched against the counter. All while his voice stayed calm and reasonable. Come on, I wanted to say, Come on Martin, let me have it. You know you want to. At least those soldiers had a chance to blow one another to pieces. Come out in the open and give it your best shot. Fight back, Martin.

He drew one ragged breath and I tensed my muscles, ready to spin around at his first sound. Without a word, he walked into the dining room. If this is war, I thought, it's cold war. Wary, cautious. Bloodless.

But of course this isn't war. Not any more. We are the survivors.

I lowered the dishes into hot water, rested my hands in liquid warmth, listened to the distant snap of soap bubbles dissolving against my wrists. From the dining room I heard Martin saying, "Dessert will just be a few minutes. Melanie, why don't you tell Grandma and Grandpa about your science project?"

I closed my lids over eyes like granite.

Martin and Melanie. Peacemakers both. Putting up the tree, stringing the lights. I considered going upstairs to Martin's study and looking through the bookshelves for *Goodbye to All That*, we have it somewhere, I'm sure. I could read Melanie's story on Christmas Eve in the soft glow of the fire and Christmas-tree lights. A kind of peace offering. But the lights on the tree look too bright and hard this year. Pagan. Mocking. And the blaze is only a fake one — gas-fed flames poking through wood that will never catch fire.

For last Christmas I started preparations in October, baking, preserving, determined to make it the best Christmas ever. One snowy Sunday, when Brenda felt up to it, she and Melanie cut out sugar-cookie trees and stars and painted them with different-coloured egg washes, while I leaned against the kitchen counter, holding my mug of coffee to my chest, and kept a careful eye on Brenda to make sure she didn't overdo it. As I watched their heads bent together in concentration, even as I listened to them squabble — "I need the red, Brenda, you've had it for *days*." "Shut up, squirt, and stop putting the brushes in all the wrong pots" — joy burned through me like brush fire.

This year Melanie set out cookie cutters and food colouring on the kitchen table, but after I walked around them for two days without mentioning them they vanished.

And her offering of the story, Christmas in the trenches, I knew what she was doing. I was the one who started the tradition, reading them one of my favourite stories every year — the presents for Marmee, the goose for Tiny Tim, the splendidly useless watch-chain and tortoiseshell comb. Finally Brenda said that if she heard one more passage from Dickens she'd roast chestnuts over the lot. From then on, she was the one who found the Christmas story, a new one every year.

I want them to stop trying so hard, all of them. Stop trying to act as though we can go on from here. At the same time, I need them to push harder, break through. Yell at me, I want to say to Melanie and Martin, I am being a bitch, I know it. And unfair, I know that too. Martin's been hurt enough. Melanie is an eleven-year-old, she shouldn't have to fight for her mother. But that's what I want them to do.

Stalemate.

White noise. Three small boys far off on the soccer field, hiding behind the snowy sledding ridge. At first I think they're hollering at one another, but now I notice that they pop up from behind the ridge, yell like crazy, then duck down as though to evade my gaze.

I am the only other person in the park.

They're yelling at me.

"You eat *dog shit!*" one of them howls, and disappears. Fits of laughter erupt from behind the ridge.

A second head pops up.

"You're a *fuck*-head!" Gone.

"You are a fuck-*brain!*" The third one pushes the second down the slope in a flurry of snow and guffaws.

Where the hell are their parents? Rage a slow burn in my chest.

"Help yourself to some *cow shit!*"

If I move towards them, they will run away squealing and victorious. If I yell at them, they will scream with delight.

If I stand absolutely still and say nothing, they will tire of this stupid game and leave me alone.

Wrong.

They shout until I can hear the hoarseness in their voices even at this distance, until the sunset has faded to a smoky twilight. At last they drag their sleds across the frozen wastes of the soccer field and head for home. If there is a God, I think (playing the game I started three years ago), they will live in one of the houses that line the field, and I will watch, I will knock on the door and tell the parents what monsters their children are. But no, they disappear down an alley. My rage has a familiar taste of helplessness. All I am doing is standing here, trying to look at a vanishing sunset. All I wanted was some vestige of hope and comfort.

God is a bastard with a vicious sense of humour.

Martin has been gone for ages. I stamp around the swings and teeter-totters, swinging my arms against my chest, bunching my fingers inside the palms of my gloves to try to bring them back to life. Brenda never played in this park. By the time we moved to the neighbourhood, seven years ago, she was eleven, and too old for such juvenile amusements. But I used to bring Melanie here a lot, and she was delighted to have me all to herself.

"We must take special comfort in Melanie now," Martin said to me after the funeral, trying to fold me in his arms.

I pushed him, hard, and threw the full weight of my fury

at him, each word cold and carefully weighed. "What exactly are you saying, Martin? We've lost one daughter but isn't it so lucky we happen to have a spare?"

His breath blew out as though I'd kicked him in the stomach. "Jesus God, Lily," he whispered, his knuckles white.

He almost hit me, then.

People have this illusion that when disaster strikes a family, the family pulls together. At any rate, I had that illusion. I had never seen death up close, imagined it like Beth's in *Little Women*, where she simply got so tired she laid down her needle and drifted away. A cheat, that's what those stories were. Marmee and her endless giving, her comforting the others when her sweetest child was stolen from her atom by atom. A cheat and a lie.

There is no mention in *Little Women* of the pain that whips the body, even under morphine. Of the horror of watching your daughter limp under the drug's influence, wearing a diaper in a grotesque parody of her first days in this world eighteen years before. Of the night sweats that turn into twenty-four-hour sweats and make even the thinnest sheet unbearable. Of how you can stare and stare at someone, watching every savage intake of breath twisting her face so that, in spite of all your care, you remember a stranger after all.

But the biggest cheat is that, when death finally arrives, it does so just out of sight. The soul slips away and you don't even see it. There is no stab to the heart, no sweeping knowledge, *She is gone*. Nothing. I keep thinking, if only I'd been fast enough, sharp enough, she would have signalled to me somehow. But no. Even the moment of death is an absence. The inhale does not occur.

Months later, I would lock my gaze onto some object — the teakettle, the piano — feeling her presence so strongly I could almost believe that, if I looked hard enough, I would catch a glimpse of her at the edge of my sight. As though she were playing a game with me, dancing just out of reach. But eventually even her presence was taken from me, and by that time I had used myself up. There wasn't anything left over for Martin or Melanie. Or even for me.

I'm freezing. I trudge up the ridge to look for Martin and stop short when I see three small bodies hunkering down on the other side of the ridge. My foul-mouthed friends from the soccer field. Making snowballs. A sled is piled with icy ammunition at the ready. And one of them, whom I take to be the ringleader, is drawing with a stick in the snow. Strategy. Plan of attack.

The boys are about ten years old, mittened, jacketed and scarved in bright colours. If I were with Martin I wouldn't give them a second thought. But I am on my own. A brief and hysterical image of being driven from the park by a flurry of snowballs makes me bite back a furious laugh. I stand my ground, hoping they are still young enough to believe in the invincibility of adults. Hoping they won't see what I see all too clearly — that I am a woman alone and weaponless, nothing to lob at them save my defiant stare.

So I stare. And they slow in their movements, poke nervously at the ground with the stick, smush a snowball back into the dead grass. I stare without smiling. Until finally the ringleader, scuffing his feet, not daring to meet my gaze, says with as much defiance as he can muster, "What?"

I've got them.

Face blank as stone, I say, "I just thought I'd come by to say hello." Still I stare. Power surges in my body, a slow burn of pleasure. I've got them, the little bastards. I carry some vestige of authority, and a slight advantage of size, and that will be enough. They are fidgeting more obviously now, demolishing the snowballs they piled up so carefully.

Over my shoulder, I see an elderly couple bring two toddlers to the swings and give them pushes. With the last traces of golden light behind them, the chinook arch above them looks protective, solicitous, and my resentment flares briefly in their direction.

The ringleader drops his stick, and all three slap the ice-balls from their mittens, then start to edge towards the swings. Very good, I think. Safety in numbers. And I begin to follow, keeping ten paces always between us. I hope your parents have filled your heads with stories of horrible things that happen to children who talk to strangers in the park, I think exultantly. I hope you are playing them through in your minds, every Clifford Olsen, every John Wayne Gacy. I hope that you've snuck downstairs to watch horror movies, and that every lengthening shadow is reminding you of grabs from behind, of screams cut short. I almost laugh out loud, but remember just in time that I don't want the couple at the swings to see me as anything other than what I appear: a woman out for a walk in a chinook on Christmas Eve.

The kids draw parallel to the playground and I feel a twinge of regret that the game will end so soon, but they don't join the family at the swings. They keep walking. Away from the playground, into the open spaces.

I can't believe it. Safety at hand, and they don't take it. But almost at the same time, I realize what they're thinking. They cannot approach the kindly couple at the swings for, after all, what can they say I have done? Simply gone up to some playing children to say hello. It's Christmas. People do all manner of silly, sentimental things during this season.

Brenda made it to Christmas. My parents arrived, as always, on the twenty-second, and I could see in their faces how much of her had already been stripped away. The effort it took her to walk to the living room on Christmas Eve scored deep tracks on her already wasted face. She had to lean against the pillows we piled on the couch in order to stay upright. But after half an hour she seemed to draw on new resources of energy, sitting straighter, raising her glass of champagne, joking with Melanie. Seeing her face flushed with laughter and champagne, I could almost make myself believe we could go on like this. Just a little more time, I pleaded with the cosmos, knowing as I did so that, even if she were to live till she was ninety, it would never be enough. Melanie sat at her feet, not saying anything, just hugging her knees to herself, sipping slowly at the half-glass of champagne we allowed her.

"Time for dinner," I said, with gaiety that, for the first time in ages, was not completely forced. And we moved to the dining room, where the tourtière was crowned with holly and the candles were ready for lighting. Still talking and laughing, Brenda rose to take the place of honour. And fell, suddenly and hard. None of us was near enough to catch her except Melanie, who could do no more than twist around beneath her to break her fall, so that she landed on her knees instead of full length.

The next day, Brenda called us in to tell us that she would have no more blood transfusions. To tell us goodbye.

The light is failing fast now, and the three boys are walking more rapidly, unsure whether to huddle close together or fan out for the best chance in case I make a run at them. I stand between them and home, safety and streetlights, forcing them farther into the frozen darkness. I'm sure they've been instructed to be home before dark, so I step after them a little faster, to put on some added pressure. I no longer feel exultant or powerful, or much of anything. I am simply following, caught up in the train of events I set in motion.

They are sidling along the fenceline now, trying to look nonchalant, trying not to draw attention to themselves. And I see they are aiming for the bike-path opening. They're smart little bastards, I have to give them that. Not tough enough to face me head-on, but smart enough to keep looking for an escape route, to stick together in the face of an enemy. I gauge the distance between me and their only way out. I could cut them off, face them down, and they know it. They stop and the ringleader whirls on me. Rips off the hat.

Long curls tumble over a bright blue parka. It's a girl, and she's terrified.

"Lily," Martin said to me countless times during that last week, "if you won't let me help you, let me get someone else to come in. A night nurse, at least." His face gaunt, his hands reaching. I'd sent my parents away the day Brenda told them goodbye.

"Don't." I left it to him to decide whether I meant don't hire a nurse, or don't touch, and walked back into the bedroom. Closed the door behind me. He and Melanie had tried to help look after Brenda, but they were too clumsy. Neither knew how to talk to her. Melanie would just lie at the foot of the bed for hours, leaning her cheek against Brenda's leg. Martin would try to keep that stiff upper lip — "You look like hell, kiddo" — voice cracking, smile twisting his face, his hand on her cheek trembling, while Brenda, my brave girl, forced an answering smile — "I feel like hell, Dad." Falling back on the pillows. You could see what it cost her. No one could look after her like I could.

She lay torpid on the bed, wearing nothing but a large diaper. I had fought against putting one on her even when she lapsed into unconsciousness, knowing how much she would hate it if she could feel it, see it, know it. But in the end I had to give in, because even under morphine she kept struggling to get up to pee into the bedpan.

"It's one of the last things to go," the visiting nurse said to me. "They just can't stand to give up control."

"Get out," I snapped, and showed her the door.

"You want to do something, Martin," I said, "you keep her away from me."

After the nurse left, I knelt close to Brenda and whispered, "It's OK, honey, you can just let it go. We don't mind, you just have to not mind too. OK?" Not mind that you are shrinking, losing breast tissue, hip and thigh, that the diaper merely sets the seal on all that's been stolen from you.

I read to her. Hours and hours. Not from the Christmas stories we used to read every year; I couldn't stand those tales where, no matter what disasters befall — debt, ghosts, poverty — everything comes out all right in the end. I read to her from letters her friends sent from college. First dates, blind dates, sororities. All the things she would never do or be. I read through rage and envy that nearly choked me. I read until I could recite the letters to her in the dark, my eyes never leaving her face, resenting any moment when I had to check back with the original text. She was being stolen from me bit by bit, and I was determined not to let one moment of her passing go unrecorded.

Two days before she died, while I was reading to her, holding her hand, she shifted slightly and my fingers brushed one of the bandages covering the blood blisters that dotted her skin. Blood poured from the wound, and I dropped the letter to grab some Kleenex and just then she had a surge of energy, trying to push herself up on one arm, saying thickly, "I have to pee."

"Honey, don't," I said. "Lie back." I tried to mop up the blood, but flicked the bandage so that blood spattered the sheet and her wasted breasts. "Oh, shit," I muttered, sponging and dabbing with the Kleenex, and the urine trickled over one of her thighs. "Oh shit, honey, I'm sorry." With enormous effort she threw her arm around my neck and leaned in close. "Don't be sorry," she whispered, almost out of hearing, and I gasped with the painful joy of hearing her speak. Not the morphine rambling, but Brenda, really speaking to me.

Melanie's white face appeared at my elbow. "Mom? Can I help? Mom?"

But I was cradling Brenda's face in my hands and staring at it as though I would never stop, searching for some sign. "Not now, Melanie," I whispered. "Not now."

The girl is about ten years old, I'd guess. She has dark eyes and hair, and round cheeks, red now with cold and defiance. Her nose is running, her eyes streaming, but she isn't crying. She looks straight at me and she says, "Leave us alone, you fucking cow." She is magnificent.

I hold her gaze for a moment, but then I make sure I look away first.

They dash for the fence, slugging each other on the back, and I hear the echoes of their laughter from the alley, their recovery swift, their victory sure. I make a mental note not to wear this parka for the next while, perhaps to avoid the park altogether for a few weeks, in case they give my description to their parents, maybe the police. I am sure their hearts are pumping madly with their close call, their breathing strong and ragged. They will tell themselves the story of their daring for days. I will perhaps become Karla Homolka, and they will be heroes. Dancing out of reach of the clutches of death.

I look out on the gathering darkness and I think, that's as much as you know. For the truly terrible thing is not death at all, but life. It is life that eats away at muscle until there is nothing left but bone beneath loose skin, life that forces spleen and liver to swell with blood cells long after the marrow has given up. It is life that makes the bargains, and whispers, It's not so bad — the dark smudges of blood beneath skin, the green bruises, collapsing veins, the monthly, then weekly, then twice-weekly blood transfusions that only gave her strength to move from her bed to a chair by the window. Even when all pretence of quality of life was stripped away — even then, life still had to be squelched and pummelled repeatedly before we — before I — could let her go.

It's almost completely dark now but, with that wonderful irony of the chinook, the wind is warmer. The ice is crisping along the edges with the fragility that comes just before thaw. I press gently with my boot, hear the splinters trace spidery cracks along the thinning surface, think of spring runoff, summer mudholes and warm mud squishing between toes.

I think about Melanie's story of the soldiers in the trenches. About the first soldier to make a move into no man's land. The kind of courage it would take to walk out there, hoping the other side would understand the signals, wouldn't blow you away with a careless round of ammunition. Or maybe the poor bugger had just gotten to the point where living and dying were all one to him. Blast away. Or not.

So I am standing in the looming darkness, watching it make a no man's land of this park, and Martin lopes into my circle of vision. Melanie resembles him more and more. Right now she is tall and thin and gawky, but eventually she will move with that loose-limbed grace. I turn and look full at Martin, at Melanie in Martin, and I hope she has also inherited his patience, his strength. I step forward, not knowing whether he will embrace me or blast me. Knowing only that it's time to lay down my arms.

When he gets here, maybe we will stand together for a moment, hold one another's empty hands. And I will hope that, somewhere in the suburbs, my mother is arguing with herself about a turkey, my father pouring himself a surreptitious whisky. Melanie has found the courage to steal into the basement. She is sneaking a frozen butter tart from its usual hiding place. She is crunching through the icy pastry with clean, white teeth, her tongue sticking to the frozen centre, resting there until it melts.

ACKNOWLEDGEMENTS

The following stories have been published previously:

"Oranges" in *Grain Magazine;* in *Two Lands, New Vision,* Coteau Books; in *Riprap,* Banff Centre Press, finalist in the Tilden Canadian Literary Prize and Fiddlehead short story competition, and was broadcast on CBC's "Alberta Anthology".

"The Gift of Tongues" in *Prairie Journal of Canadian Literature.*

"Lifeguard" in *Alberta Rebound,* NeWest Press; in *Canadian Stories,* Prentice Hall; and in the *Issues Collection* series, McGraw-Hill Ryerson.

"The Quick" in *Prairie Fire.*

"Minor Alterations" in *Dandelion Magazine* (winner, short fiction competition); and in Prairie Anthology *Due West,* Coteau Books, NeWest and Turnstone Presses.

I thank the Alberta Foundation for the Arts and the Canada Council for their support. I am very grateful to the various writing programs, some government funded, some privately funded, that taught me so much about the craft of writing: the University of Calgary creative writing program, Humber College, the Markin-Flanagan Writer-in-Residence program, the Banff Writing Studio, the Sage Hill Writing Experience, and the Crowsnest Writing Retreat.

Most of all I am grateful to the extraordinarily generous writing community that I inhabit, and to the friends who "kept me at it". Special thanks to Betty and Sue for being there in the eleventh hour, and to Keith for seeing me through all the others.

REFERENCES

Stanley Milgram, "Some Conditions of Obedience and Disobedience to Authority", *Human Relations Journal*, Vol. 18, 1965, pp. 57-75.

Francis Thompson, "The Hound of Heaven", *The Norton Anthology of English Literature*, Volume 2, 5th edition. M.H. Abrams, General Editor. New York: W.W. Norton & Co., 1986, pp. 1710-1714.

Peter Tompkins and Christopher Bell, *The Secret Life of Plants*. New York York: Harper & Row, 1973.

Dr. Dennis Waitley, *The Psychology of Winning: Ten Qualities of a Total Winner*. New York: Berkley Books, 1984. (Copyright Dr. Waitley, 1979).